Red, like my bleeding heart in your hand

A Wildflowers of Deliverance novella
by

Sarah B. Elisa

This is a work of fiction. Similarities to real people, places, or events
are entirely coincidental.

RED, LIKE MY BLEEDING HEART IN YOUR HAND

Written by Sarah B. Elisa
Edited by Ember Hood
Cover photo by Natalie Parham, Unsplash
Interior art by Sketchify, Canva

ISBN: 979-8991930208 (ebook)
ISBN: 979-8991930215 (paperback)
Library of Congress Control Number: 2025904324

First edition. February 19, 2025.

This one is for everybody who said they'd read anything I wrote. Time to pony up :)

Table of Contents

Chapter One: The new kid 1
Chapter Two: The creek 10
Chapter Three: The devil 19
Chapter Four: The hypocrite 25
Chapter Five: The loft 33
Chapter Six: The garage 39
Chapter Seven: The wrong thing 45
Chapter Eight: The world tips 53
Chapter Nine: His perfect day 62
Chapter Ten: Beautiful and good 72
Chapter Eleven: Fundamental 80
Chapter Twelve: All he ever wanted 91
Chapter Thirteen: On top of the world 96

CHAPTER ONE

The new kid

The new kid is red-faced and wheezing by the time they make it up the hill. It ain't even half as big as the one over by Chuck's place, but by the way Teddy is huffing and puffing, you'd think he'd run up and down it a dozen times.

Before he can think better of it, Nash asks, "What's wrong with you?"

He ain't fat, not even close. He probably ain't a smoker neither, considering most six-year-olds aren't, but he's sure breathin' like one. Maybe this is why Ms. Rainer was fixed on having Nash see Teddy home from the bus stop. Somehow, she knew just by looking, that there's somethin' off with this one.

As Teddy heaves for air, his backpack slips free from one shoulder, but he shrugs it back on and keeps dragging his feet through the gravel. His house is visible now, set too close to the road, so it's a muted dusty gray under all the gravel dust. The dust swirls in the wind like a toddler playing at being a ballerina after too much sugar, and the leaves dance along to the rasp of the corn stalks shifting and swaying in time.

Nash hesitates on the porch as Teddy throws open the storm door and pushes into the house without a backward glance. When he doesn't close the door behind him, Nash follows.

Inside, Teddy's ragged breaths are louder, helped along to Nash's ears by the uncovered wood floor. He follows into the kitchen where the yellowy linoleum pops and crackles underfoot in the places where it's bubbled up.

The drawer beside the sink opens with a screech of wood as Teddy pulls out an inhaler, puts it between his lips, and sucks in a long, deep breath. With his eyes closed and his face screwed up, he lowers the inhaler and holds his breath for a long, long time. Then he exhales, wipes his nose with the back of his hand, and faces Nash with his chin tipped up proudly.

"All the things."

"Huh?"

"You asked what's wrong with me," Teddy says in a reedy voice. He pauses to breathe. "There's a lot wrong with me."

"Oh. Are you... sick?"

Dying is what he wants to ask, but he's been whacked in the back of the head enough to know better.

Teddy shrugs, inhaler between his lips again and Nash has to wait until he tosses the inhaler back in the drawer, rams it shut, and exhales.

"Not right now," Teddy says, "but maybe tomorrow. Wanna play Pokémon?" He flips the lid off a sagging women's shoe box on the table and reveals a treasure trove of Pokémon cards.

Nash cranes for a closer look before he can stop himself. "Woah, those are all yours?"

He pulls cards out by the handful. "Yeah, my mom and dad used to buy me a pack every time they had to travel."

Nash stares, mesmerized, as Teddy rifles through the cards like he knows what he's looking at—all the colors and creatures and elements—it's overwhelming.

"They must travel a lot." He can't imagine what that's like. The farthest he's ever been from Deliverance is the Walmart in Buford Hills, the next town over.

"Used to. They're dead now, so..." He keeps messing with the cards. Like it's nothing to him. Like he doesn't care. Like his face isn't scrunched and his shoulders aren't boxed up around his ears.

If he wasn't so visibly uncomfortable, Nash would think he was trying to make a joke. He doesn't know what to say, so, out of pity, he puts his backside on the line and asks, "How do we play?"

He's gonna get an ass whoopin' for being home late, but it's almost worth it for the relieved smile that overtakes Teddy's discomfort as he babbles about types and strengths and weaknesses.

Nash settles himself opposite him at the table and silently bemoans his inability to ignore the kicked puppy types.

"Thank you, Mr. Spinoza, but I'd rather walk."

"Are you sure?"

Teddy's uncle is a middle kind of man. He isn't tall or short. Nor is he skinny or fat. Neither smiley nor angry. He seems content to hold the middle of it all. He's got his car keys in his hand and is poised over a pair of mangy boots, waiting for Nash's change of heart. He ain't even out of his shop uniform yet—streaked with car gunk though it is.

"I can drop you off and have a quick word with your folks explaining why you were out late. It's nearly dark."

"You don't need to," Nash rushes to say. "Honest. I walk quick 'n' it ain't far."

His aren't the kind of parents anybody likes to meet. Maybe Mama'd be alright without Daddy stompin' and ragin' all the time, but she ain't without him so there's nothin' for it 'cept to keep the middle kind of men away from Daddy's all-the-way kind of man.

Mr. Spinoza's expression is mild as he watches Nash, but Nash gets the feeling he's seeing through to the heart of things and Mr. Spinoza knows exactly why Nash don't want anybody reasonable near his daddy.

He doesn't move or breathe until Mr. Spinoza nods. Only the wrinkle between his eyebrows betrays his discomfort with the plan, and Nash means to be long gone before that discomfort can win him over.

"You'd better get a move on then."

"Yes, sir."

"You're going to be in trouble?"

Teddy's wavering question stops Nash's inching retreat toward the door. He's wearing the same bafflement that all the kids with good, kind parents display whenever they're exposed to someone who can't blindly trust their folks.

"Only a little." And maybe in another life that'd be the truth. It's not late, but it's the time of year when the sun turns in early and only rises when it can't get away with staying down any longer. And Daddy don't usually need an excuse to put the fear of God into him, so it's always a special treat when Nash gives him one.

"Why'd you stay then?"

It might be something in the jutting tip of Teddy's chin or the proud shine in his eyes, or perhaps it's instinct honed from years of tiptoeing around his old man that warns Nash away from the truth—or at least the truth Teddy's diggin' for.

"I never seen that many Pokémon cards before."

Teddy's posture relaxes, and that same playful grin from earlier peeps out.

"Have," Mr. Spinoza says.

Baffled, Nash retorts, "Have not."

Mr. Spinoza shakes his head. "No, 'I *have never* seen that many Pokémon cards before.'"

Nash glances at Teddy, then looks back to Mr. Spinoza and slowly, with his best enunciation, says, "Neither have I."

Teddy cackles, head thrown back, and nearly falls from his seat at the table. Mr. Spinoza smiles, and it lightens him up, but not enough to make Nash feel better about being the butt of some joke he doesn't understand.

He inches back. "I should go."

"Thank you for keeping Teddy company. You're welcome back anytime—but call home and get permission first."

"Yes, sir." But he knows there ain't no way Daddy'll ever give him permission to come back. He shoots a longing glance at the cards still strewn across the table. It's a shame he won't get to play again. It was fun while it lasted.

Nash sets his tray in front of him and eases onto the bench. Once he's sitting, he breathes out slowly through the ache in his ribs as his body acclimates to the new position. Then he nearly drops his pizza when a lunch box slams onto the table across from him and a small body throws itself onto the bench.

"I made you a deck." Teddy doesn't explain what that means and upends his lunch box on the table. Out falls a plastic wrapped sandwich, a baggie of baby carrots, a box of apple juice, and two stacks of Pokémon cards. Teddy sets the deck that's bound by a blue rubber band besides Nash's tray, then removes the pink scrunchie from the other and puts it around his wrist.

He glances at Nash's pizza, held aloft and uneaten. "Hurry up and eat that or we won't have time to play."

Unsure what else to do, Nash takes a bite. He swallows. "Aren't you gonna eat?"

Teddy makes a face but dutifully unwraps his sandwich and takes a bite before setting it aside and turning his attention back to shuffling his cards.

Nash makes a face at the sandwich as it oozes purple on the discarded plastic wrap. "Is that just jelly?" It explains why he doesn't seem interested in eating it. Then again, it's weird that he brought a lunch at all. Everybody knows Fridays are pizza days and nobody wants cold lunch instead of pizza.

"I'm allergic to peanut butter and we're all out of turkey." With his tongue between his lips, he attempts a real shuffle, like how adults do, and drops his cards all over the table.

Nash rescues one from the edge and slides it back to him. "Why not have pizza then?"

"Allergic."

"To *pizza*?"

"Cheese and tomatoes." He eyes Nash's slice wistfully before he smears his cards around to get them good and mixed up. "It smells good, though."

"Oh." Nash recalls their walk yesterday and how he went straight to his inhaler once they got inside. How during their walk was the only time he'd been quiet. "What else are you allergic to?"

Teddy's annoyance is clear in the sharp rapping of his cards against the table and the pucker of his lips. "Do you want to talk about all the stuff that's wrong with me, or do you want to play? We don't have time for both."

"Play." He crams a massive bite into his mouth and chews as he opens his chocolate milk.

Teddy mimics him with a similarly large bite of his jelly sandwich and says through his full mouth, "You like the electric types, right?" He swallows thickly. "I gave you all the ones I could find, but there's not a lot, so I gave you the flying and psychic types too. Is that okay?"

"Yeah, that's fine." He shoves the last of his pizza in his mouth and wipes his hands vigorously on his jeans before he picks up the deck of cards Teddy prepared for him. "Did you get all fighting ones again?"

"I added some ground ones." He looks up and grins. "Ground is super effective against electric."

"So? Aren't flying and psychic super effective against fighting?"

Teddy lights up. "You remembered."

"How to kick your butt? 'Course I did."

"Well, this time you won't. I've got a plan."

They don't finish the match before the bell rings, but Nash had Teddy on the ropes no matter what Teddy says about late game comebacks.

That afternoon, Teddy pulls a red handkerchief up over his mouth and nose before they get off the bus and keeps both arms over his face until the cloud of dust kicked up by the departing bus blows away. His voice is muffled behind the fabric, but he chatters all the way to his house and doesn't stop until Nash hesitates at the end of his driveway.

"Aren't you coming?" He peers at him through fogged lenses. "I want a rematch so I can show you how I was going to win."

Nash shakes his head. "I gotta get home."

"Oh." Teddy doesn't bother hiding his disappointment. "Well, what about tomorrow? That's your house, right?" He points at the roof in the distance, peeking just over the hill that obscures most of their property. "I can come over and—"

"No! I mean, I'll come here. If I can, I mean. I have to ask."

"Okay," Teddy says slowly. "Why don't you want anybody at your house?" He gestures at the dusty house behind him. "It's not like we're rich or anything. You don't have to be embarrassed."

What's embarrassing is that he clocked their lack of money without ever stepping through their front door, but that ain't it. "I'm not *embarrassed*," Nash snaps. "I just don't want to deal with how annoying my sister will be with you around. That's all."

Teddy's expression clears. "You have a sister?"

"Yeah, an annoying one. She'll be in kindergarten next year, so we'll have to deal with her at school then."

"Cool, maybe she can play with us, and we can do three-way battles! I've never done one of those before."

Nash shakes his head. "She's not smart enough. She'll just get in the way and mess up your cards. I'll just come over here, okay? If Mama says it's alright, I mean."

Teddy has a look like he wants to argue some more, so Nash waves and starts backing up the way he came.

"See you tomorrow."

"Yeah, okay. See you."

Relieved he got out of that, Nash turns on his heel and hurries home. Midway down the hill, he looks back, but Teddy is gone.

CHAPTER TWO

The creek

Nash is up before the sun to get his chores done and be gone before Jo gets up. That way, she can't insist on following him. Mama waves him off without questions when he explains he'll be spending the day at the creek. She'll need at least one more cup of coffee before she's up to talkin', and by then she'll be off to her shift at the diner in town. He hopes she remembers to tell Daddy where he's at, so he don't get mad later when he can't find him. Ain't no way he's wakin' him up to say it himself, though.

He doesn't think nothin' of the time until after he knocks on the Teddy's front door and a rumpled lady with long, long hair opens it barefoot in nothing but a fluffy polka dot robe.

He pulls his shoulders back and tucks his hands behind

his back. "Sorry, ma'am. I was wonderin' if Teddy could come out 'n' play."

She frowns, glances past him to where the sun is in the fight of its life to make it over the horizon, and then looks back down. "He's asleep."

"Oh. Well, when's he usually up?"

"On a Saturday? We'll be lucky to see him before noon."

"Noon?" Christ on a cracker. What's he supposed to do until *noon*? "I... Well, I suppose I can come back."

Finally, a tired smile tickles the corners of her mouth. "Tell you what, you come back at nine-thirty and I'll make sure he's ready for you."

"You don't have to—"

"It'll be good for him. It's Nash, right? Is that short for Nashville?"

He's not sure if he succeeds at smothering his distaste. Technically, it's short for Nash Motors, but he doesn't tell anybody that, and it's only his daddy that cares, anyhow.

"Just Nash," he says.

"Alright, Nash. I'm Julie. We really appreciate you including Teddy. He's had a hard time recently, and this move wasn't easy on him."

Nash frowns. He doesn't like how Teddy's uncle and now his aunt have thanked him for giving Teddy the time of day. He's not *that* annoying. Better than Jo at any rate. By "hard time," does she mean his parents dying? That's why he had to move here, right? He can't think of why else he'd suddenly join his aunt and uncle in the Middle of Nowhere, Tennessee.

"Sure, Mrs. Spinoza." He takes a step back. "I'll be back in a couple hours."

She waves him goodbye with an expression that seems

indecisive, but he can't think of a reason to hang around—
even if she wasn't a strange adult in her pajamas.

"I thought we were going to play Pokémon."

"We can, I guess, but aren't you worried your cards will
get ruined?"

"No?" Teddy shoots him a look over the top of the red
handkerchief tied around the bottom half of his face and then
kicks a bit of gravel. "We'd just play at the table like normal."

Inside? It made sense to play inside when it was just
them, but now that the adults are home... Wouldn't they get
annoyed?

"I'll show you the creek. It'll be fun."

"What's a crick?"

"A creek? You know..." He makes a fishlike motion with
his hand. "Water? A river, but real little?"

"Oh, a *creek*. What's so fun about a creek?"

He doesn't bother explaining since, despite his
grumblings, Teddy follows him.

Nash splits from the road, turning down a narrow trail
that cuts through the cornfield separating his house from
Teddy's. Under the shade of the waving stalks, the wind cuts
out and they tromp along the uneven dirt as dry, coarse
leaves whip at their faces.

"Is this even legal?" Teddy smacks at a broken stalk and
gets knocked in the nose for his trouble. "Whose corn is this?"

"Chuck's dad owns the land, but they live way down the
road over that big hill with the helicopter trees. Chuck said
they put off harvest 'till next week on account of not wantin'

to miss the spelling bee, so we don't gotta worry about the combine comin' 'round just yet."

"Who's Chuck?"

"Big guy that sits next to me. The one that got all mad when I finished the addition tables before him, even though I always do."

"Oh yeah. At recess, he told everyone you cheated."

Nash snorts. Chuck would. He's not used to losing. He dominates at everything: basketball, kickball, four square, tetherball, spelling bees, and fitting the most jumbo marshmallows in his mouth. But he can't touch math because Nash refuses to dumb himself down to make it easy for him. If Chuck wants it, he's gonna have to take it from him.

"*Did* you cheat?"

Nash jerks to a stop and whirls around.

Teddy nearly crashes into him as he stumbles. This close, it's more obvious than ever how small Teddy is. The top of his head barely meets Nash's nose and Nash thinks he could fold himself in half hot dog–style and still have breadth left over to outstrip the width of Teddy's shoulders.

Despite this, Teddy lifts his chin and stares up at him from behind breath-fogged glasses without an ounce of nerves.

"I don't cheat."

"Never?"

"I don't need to. I'm the best at math. You can ask anyone."

Anyone besides Chuck.

Teddy tips his head to the side and considers him. "Not anymore. I was the best at my school, so I bet I will be here too."

Nash scoffs. He doesn't mean to be mean, but math is the

one thing at school that he doesn't need to try at. Words can be difficult, especially sounding them out, but numbers are easy. Numbers make sense. Nobody is better at math than he is and everyone, except Chuck, knows it and allows him his crown uncontested.

"It's true," Teddy insists. "I even finished my test before you."

"No, you didn't." He would have noticed someone else walking up to the front of the room before him. He's always the first to make that walk to Ms. Rainer's desk to turn his test in.

"At my old school, we flipped ours over and put our pencils down. Then the teacher came around and collected them."

"Then how did you know who was fastest?"

He shrugs. "I don't think that was the point."

That doesn't make any sense. Why time the test if not to see who outstrips everyone else and who struggles to keep up? He shakes his head. "It doesn't matter. You still weren't first."

"I *was*. I just didn't know what I was supposed to do until other kids were getting up."

Nash makes a sound of disbelief in his throat and turns around to continue their walk.

"Hey!"

Something small and bony strikes him between his shoulder blades. Incredulous, he turns around and finds Teddy glaring up at him from his tiptoes with his hands in fists at his sides.

"I *am* better than you, and I'll prove it. When's the next timed test?"

"Did you hit me?"

He jerks his chin up and glares over the top of his handkerchief. "When is it?"

"Thursday. Every Thursday."

"What about subtraction?"

"We don't start subtraction until after Christmas."

Teddy exhales a scoffing laugh and relaxes to the flats of his feet. "Oh, then I'll definitely beat you. We started subtraction weeks ago at my old school."

Nash narrows his eyes, but Teddy's fit of temper seems to have left him as swiftly as it arrived.

His eyes crinkle in the corners as he lightly whacks Nash's arm. "Are you gonna show me this *crick* or what?"

"Are you makin' fun of how I talk?"

"I like how you talk."

Nash frowns at him. He'd believe it if not for the way Teddy and his uncle laughed at him the other day. He still doesn't understand what they found funny, but he knows it was something he said.

"Don't look like that." Teddy rocks back on his heels. "I like how you say *'lectric* and *mama* and now *crick*. Are we going or not?"

Nash observes him for a beat longer, but he seems earnest. Without a word, Nash turns and continues leading the way to the... the *creek*. He's never been too good at letting go of the anger that sometimes balls up in his chest like a nasty old hairball, but the very last thing he ever wants to be is like his daddy, so he swallows back the mean-spirited words that want to choke out of him. Meanwhile Teddy chatters about nothing of consequence all the way through the cornfield, over the ridge, and down past the tree line where a little bubbling spit of water curls around hills and through tree roots.

It's too cold to strip to bare feet and splash around, but Nash shows Teddy the tree that fell and now forms a bridge between banks. They challenge each other to cross it first by walking, then hopping on one foot, then galloping like a horse. Teddy slips while skipping and lands in the creek with a splash that soaks up to his knees, but he scrambles out with a wheezing laugh and orders Nash to do a cartwheel.

That laugh should have been Nash's first clue, but he's caught up in the contest now, anger forgotten as he pushes himself to keep up with Teddy's demands. He beams as he completes the cartwheel and then tells Teddy to hop like a frog. It's only when the coughing starts that he realizes something is wrong.

Teddy sits on the bank with his face in his folded arms as he hacks and wheezes. When he sits up, his eyes are streaming and what Nash can see of his face is flushed and puckered with sweat even though the air is cool.

"Are you alright?"

"The handkerchief... was supposed... to help." He punches the ground in frustration. "I have to... go home."

"Alright. I'll walk with you."

Teddy rips up a handful of grass and hurls it ineffectively at the creek. As the blades flutter to rest atop the water, he pushes to his feet.

Together, they trudge back the way they came. The walk to the creek was full of chatter but the walk back is silent except for Teddy's shallow, wheezing breaths. Halfway up the ridge, Teddy has to stop for a break as he coughs and catches his breath. Then they stop again at the top so he can deal with the snot streaming from his nose. And again just outside the cornfield for another coughing fit.

Worry is a nagging tickle in his belly as Nash shifts his

weight and Teddy hunkers over his knees and wheezes. It takes a long time for Teddy to catch his breath this time. Lots longer than all the times before.

"C'mere," Nash demands soon as Teddy's complexion drains from red to pink. "We gotta get you out of this air, I think."

Teddy doesn't argue, he just loops his little stick arms around Nash's neck and weakly clambers onto his back. That scares Nash worse than anything else.

He goes fast as he can without trippin' buns over ears on the tricky knobbles and roots stickin' up in the cornfield.

It ain't bad 'till they get to the road. The ditch is steep and as soon as they get close, Teddy's breathing gets real, real strange. Nash can feel it vibrate through Teddy's chest against his back as Teddy struggles to get air in through too small a pipe. Nash'd be scrambling on all fours if he could, but he's got Teddy, so he struggles to keep his feet from slidin' too much on the crumbling dirt and rocks and climbs.

Once he's on the road, it's better for him, but not so much for Teddy what with all the dust his shufflin' feet kick up.

They must've seen him comin' up the drive, because soon as Nash steps onto the porch, the door bangs open and Mr. and Mrs. Spinoza come chargin' out of it.

Mr. Spinoza scoops Teddy from Nash's back right quick, then looks to Mrs. Spinoza with a frightful face.

"Hospital," Mrs. Spinoza says. "Now."

"Get the keys and my wallet," Mr. Spinoza says. "Don't forget the inhaler."

There's a whirlwind of movement and pitched urgent tones as Mr. Spinoza gets Teddy in the car and Mrs. Spinoza rushes in and out of the house, pausing only to crush Nash in a surprise hug before she departs with an even more surprising kiss to the top of his head. Then their old gray sedan is spittin' rocks as they tear down the road. Nash watches from the porch thinkin' he mighta just done in his first and only friend.

CHAPTER THREE

The devil

Nash waits on Teddy's front porch until the sun settles on the horizon and his belly is yowling about missing lunch, then he kicks gravel all the way home. He'll try them again tomorrow, he decides. They should be back by tomorrow.

He slips through the front door and, quiet as can be, toes off his old ratty sneakers that are one size too small.

Daddy's got the news on again. There's been lots of blathering about some billionaire that's wantin' to live in space. Daddy says he's gonna change the world, but Mama says ain't nothin' gonna change for folks like us. Nash figures she's got the right of it. How can some guy going up to space fix any of his problems? Whether he makes it or not, he's still gotta go to school, and come home, and tiptoe past the living room lest Daddy catch sight of him and decide it's been too long since he's expressed his opinion on his backside.

Try as he might to keep 'em quiet, the stairs always give him away. So he goes up quick as he dares and darts into his room before he can hear whether Daddy got up from his chair.

"Nashery Owens, just where have you been?"

He jumps, but it's only Jo standin' on his bed with her dolls all around her and her hands on her hips.

Her hair is thick, dark, and twisted into frizzy braids on either side of her head. She's got freckles like him, but hers are neat and contained over the bridge of her nose like the kids on TV, not like the explosion that's all over his face and shoulders and throat. She's round, even for an almost five-year-old. Her birthday's comin' up right before Thanksgiving and she won't shut up about how that means she'll finally be old enough to follow him along to school. That means takin' the bus together, shooing her off during lunch, dodging her at recess, and then getting back on the bus with her. He's tired just thinking about it.

"You know that ain't my name."

"It's not fair Mama gets to lay into me with a *trouble name* while you get to be just Nash all the time, so I've set out to make things right."

"That's stupid."

"*You're* stupid. Why were you gone all day? Don't you know how boring it is here all alone?"

"I was at the creek."

She flounces down. "Next year I'll be allowed at the creek, and you'll never be rid of me."

"That's why I gotta get my freedom while I can."

"Whatever. You're just in time for the coronation. You wanna be Delilah again?"

"Is she the killer?"

Jo smiles, wicked sharp despite her cherub cheeks. "That's the treat. They're all killers, but only Juliet's got it figured out."

She always has some kind of antic going on. He wonders if it's a deficiency because of how they're being raised, or if it's just how she is and was always gonna be no matter how lucky her draw for parents was.

He kneels opposite her on the bed and picks up Delilah. She's technically a Ken doll, but according to Jo, she feels more at home wearing makeup and dresses like the girls. Nash doesn't particularly care what he calls the dolls or what they look like, but he thinks Delilah is the most interesting. He'd never tell Jo, but he knows what it's like to hide himself away, and he's jealous that Delilah gets to be as weird and different as she feels on the inside.

Well... she does so long as Daddy isn't around. He ain't allowed to play with the dolls, but if Daddy caught him playing with girl toys *and* saw that one of 'em was a boy all gussied up like a girl, well...

He'd be sore again at school, that's for sure.

They play quiet as they can 'cept for a little ruckus when the queen-to-be collapses with the crown in her hands.

Shortly after, the stairs creak and they go dead silent until Daddy's footsteps pass the door and continue on down to his and Mama's room. They sit still and quiet until the big box fan turns on. Only then does Nash venture down to the kitchen and slap together a plate of sandwiches quick as he can, stomach grumbling all empty 'n' hollow.

Jo lays down not long after they eat and ends up driftin' off in his bed like usual.

He stays up a bit longer, sitting in the window, trying to

catch lights at the house up the hill, but the horizon stays dark.

When Mama's headlights turn up the drive, he shuts off the light quick and dives into bed beside Jo. He's gotta kick her 'till she rolls closer to the wall and lets him in, then he hikes the blanket up under his chin and squeezes his eyes shut as Mama's footsteps start up the stairs.

The door opens just wide enough to let in the sweet, fried smell of the diner and a beam of light right onto his face. He don't breathe until Mama shuts the door and slips back down the stairs to move around in the kitchen.

Sometimes he wonders how different things would be if Mama loved them enough to take them away from Daddy. He supposes that kind of love would come along with being tucked in and kissed goodnight. Maybe even checked on with words rather than secret peeks when she thinks they're not awake to know about it. He asked his Sunday school teacher how come, if God's love is forever and always and no matter what, why he doesn't save them from the bad stuff. She didn't like that much. Said it's the devil that makes the bad and God makes the good.

But Nash doesn't think that's quite right. He thinks God is a lot like Mama—lovin' so long as it's from a distance and you don't think too much about what he could fix if he really tried. The sticky questions are always smoothed over with pretty words like, "Do what's right even when it's hard," and "Learn to fight your own battles." His teacher says it's inspiring, but all he hears is that as far as fightin' the devil goes, he's on his own. Honestly, he wouldn't be surprised to find there is no God up there pokin' people to do what's right.

But he's got no issue believin' in the devil. Not only is the devil real, he's mean as spit and sleeps just down the hall.

He keeps watch on the Spinoza's house all day Sunday but the gray sedan only returns once around midmorning and by the time he's rushed up the hill, it's gone again and don't come back—even though he stays up long after Jo is snoring into his pillow and Mama gets her goodnight lookin' in.

By Wednesday, he's sure Teddy is dead.

He gets so bold as to ask Ms. Rainer if Teddy'll be comin' back, but she just smiles at him all sweet like adults do to babies when they burble nonsense and dribble spit down their fronts. She tells him Teddy'll be back soon, and it's wonderful to see that he finally made a friend.

He comes away from the conversation with no comfort as to Teddy's health and rankled by the idea that he's known for being a friendless loser. Hasn't anyone figured out yet that it's on purpose? *On purpose* he doesn't collect extra pairs of grasping hands that need things he can't give. *On purpose* he keeps his distance.

Yet here he is, checkin' on the new kid that lives in the house up the hill and fretting over all the nothin' he's heard about the state of him.

When Nash walks into the classroom on Thursday morning and sees Teddy sitting in his usual spot—a little paler and more rundown than before, but breathing on his own—relief nearly cuts his legs out from under him. He takes his moment to feel it and turn his head back on straight, then he sits down and takes out the word search they started yesterday.

Just because something in his heart betrayed his decision to not let anyone too close doesn't mean he has to act any different.

Relief hits him all over again when Teddy sits across from him at lunch, already chattering on about their timed test this afternoon like nothing happened. Nash follows Teddy's lead and tells him he's gonna finish so far ahead of him Ms. Rainer'll send him up a grade and demote Teddy down to kindergarten with Jo.

She doesn't, but that doesn't stop them from spending the next four years fighting to outperform the other. It's only when Teddy turns his efforts to fighting others that things get complicated.

CHAPTER FOUR

The hypocrite

Hey, geek! Your backpack is open. Oops! My bad."

Nash follows the jeering pitch of Chuck's voice through the crowd around the tetherball pole, elbowing anyone who doesn't get out of his way quick enough. The other kids don't make it easy for him.

"Here's the dog!" a girl crows and someone shoves Nash from behind.

He keeps his feet and his focus and pushes through despite the way the other kids try to link up to keep him out. He tumbles into the clear space where Chuck has Teddy backed up against a wall of toothy smiles, sharp with anticipation. Several of them sour as they register Nash's arrival and a few even turn and leave, disappointed.

"Back off, ugly!" Teddy shouts. The contents of his backpack are spilled around his feet, more Pokemon cards than school supplies. "I could kick your ass if I wanted!"

Nash swallows a sigh. Teddy never knows when to keep his mouth shut.

Chuck takes a menacing step forward and lifts one big meaty fist. Teddy, the idiot, sneers up at him from a foot below, feet braced apart and knobby knuckles up around his face—like Chuck couldn't knock his rock-solid head clean off his shoulders in one blow if he really put his mind to it.

Nash steps between them. "Leave off, Chuck." He pushes back against Teddy and the stubborn idiot nearly tips over rather than back away. "You know it ain't a fair fight."

"The hell it's not!" Teddy spits.

Chuck cracks his knuckles and his narrowed eyes don't leave Teddy where he's trying to duck around Nash's arm. "I dunno why you always stick up for him. You heard what he said. He wants a fight."

"You bet your ass I—" Teddy's breath punches out of him as Nash's elbow slams into his stomach.

"You got your fun in." Nash gestures at Teddy's things strewn over the blacktop. "Ain't that enough?"

Chuck looks at him then, blue eyes bright and bewildered under a shock of orange fringe. Then again, he always looks kind of bewildered in a just-rolled-out-of-bed sort of way.

He looks like he's gearing up to argue, so Nash tries a different track. "Won't Mr. Blackthorn be lookin' for you if you're not on the field soon?"

Chuck glowers. "I know what you're doin'," he mutters. "You know he *asks* for this crap, right?"

Nash lowers his voice. "You hit harder, but you know

I'm quick. You really wanna face the rest of the team with a busted lip?"

"Just beat up those nerds!" someone in the crowd shouts, followed by a general cry of agreement.

Chuck glares at the crowd, annoyed. "I have good grades, too. They're not the only smart kids."

"Yeah," a girl says, "but you're not *weird*."

Chuck works his jaw and Nash prepares his elbow in case Teddy gets the hankering to jump back into the boiling pot.

He doesn't need to.

With a bitter curl to his lip, Chuck hocks a loogie not an inch from the toe of Nash's sneaker and whirls away. The crowd surges back to let him through and the stasis spell breaks. A few of the bolder kids kick at Teddy's books as they leave and Nash has to get a real good grip on his sleeve to keep Teddy from tearin' after them and kickin' up a whole new batch of troubles.

Once they've got some space, he crouches and scrabbles to collect Teddy's things. "Help me, would you? If we miss the bus again, we'll have to walk and won't have time to go to the creek."

Teddy whips his open bag off his back and stoops to let Nash cram his things inside. Low and sore, he says, "I didn't need you to butt in. I had it under control."

Nash keeps quiet.

In the years he's known Teddy, he's learned the best way to handle his bouts of aggression is to let him wear himself out. Any interaction only fuels his temper and pushes him to take things further. It's a dance Nash is uncomfortably familiar with. Sometimes he wonders what about him is so damaged that he'd choose to hang onto someone like Teddy

—all fire and fury—when his daddy is the same except all cold where Teddy runs hot.

He hikes Teddy's backpack onto his shoulder alongside his own. "I'll run ahead and get the driver to wait." He knows what kind of look that comment will earn him, so he doesn't look and instead turns tail and runs.

The whole ride home is silent except for Jo's yammerin' on about what took them so long. She lays over the back of their seat as she implies what they could've been gettin' up to in a lonely dark corner just the two of 'em but Nash has heard worse from the other kids and she don't say it in that mean-spirited way they do, anyway. So he keeps quiet and lets her talk and Teddy sulk until the doors open on their empty stretch of gravel.

Teddy waits to unload his troubles until they're outside the dust cloud of the bus's departure in a barren cornfield and Nash has gotten rid of Jo with a lie about Mama needin' her for yard work. His handkerchief muffles his speech and his steamed glasses hide the exact furious squint of his eyes, but Nash has been privy to enough of his tirades to sketch out the missing details himself. He lets Teddy go on by himself for a while before he finally says something Nash feels is worth addressing.

"You don't always have to swoop in and save me, you know. I can handle Chuck. I had ten bullies just like him at my old school and nobody there ever got in my way."

"Must not've had any friends."

Teddy jerks to a stop and spins to face him. "What did you say?"

The field around them is littered with yellowed scraps of cornstalks. The dim afternoon light struggles through the overcast sky to warm the thawing earth. It's what Nash has come to think of as the sweet spot between winter and spring. When the air is no longer so thin and chilled that it sets off Teddy's asthma, but before all the greenery springs back to life and turns the air hostile with pollen.

It's the only time of year Teddy can play with him at the creek without dying, and they'll only get a handful of weeks before they have to retreat indoors and keep out of the adults' way. He knows that's Teddy's preference, but he'd rather not squander their scant afternoons of freedom arguing about dumb stuff like whether he should let Teddy get the snot beat out of him.

"You heard right," Nash says. He has to look down to meet Teddy's furious stare. While Nash has grown a smattering of inches, he swears Teddy hasn't grown a millimeter since they met. "If you had one real friend back in your precious city, you'd've never had to face down ten bullies on your own. If I see you in trouble, then I'm gonna be in trouble right along with you. You can spit nails at me all you want, but you won't change my mind."

Teddy grits his teeth. "You're a hypocrite, Nash."

Nash scoffs. "Hypocrite" was one of their vocabulary words last month and ever since, Teddy has been throwing it around like a roll of quarters at an arcade.

"You are," Teddy insists. "You try to fight all my fights for me, but don't let me help you with yours."

"That's 'cuz I don't have any fights 'cept the ones you start, dingus. You're the one that goes 'round taking swings at anything that looks at you funny."

"Then let's go hang out at your house."

Nash goes still.

Like a hound caught up in the scent of his prey, Teddy leans in until Nash can make out the earth-brown of his eyes glaring through his fogged lenses.

"How come I've never been to your house? Don't lie. You're stupid if you think I haven't figured it out."

Nash's voice comes out distant to his own ears. "That's different."

"How?" Teddy demands. "A bully's a bully, if you ask me. No matter how big they are."

Because it's real, Nash wants to say, but he doesn't. Teddy won't like it if he implies that his troubles at school aren't real, but the fact is, Nash has no escape from his bully. His bully has control and power over him in a way Teddy's bullies, no matter how numerous, never will. He can't go home to get away. The only place he has that feels safe—in the way a home should—is the creek.

"Let me help with your bully, and I'll let you help with mine." Teddy sticks out his hand like a gentleman's agreement is enough to protect him, like the skinny little asthmatic with a million and one allergies is any match for his old man.

Yet...

Despite his deficiencies, there's an unshakable confidence in Teddy that's difficult to look past. It's tricky because Teddy always means what he says, but Nash likes to think he's gotten pretty good at telling when he's talking bullshit and when he might actually be onto something. The other problem is, once you spend enough time with Teddy, some of that baseless confidence sheds off onto you when you're not lookin'. Like glitter, you don't realize it's there until it catches the light just right.

Nash takes Teddy's hand and grips it how Daddy taught him at church for greetin' time. Nobody smacks him in the back of the head for doin' it wrong, even though Teddy doesn't pump his hand up and down and he holds on far longer than he should. He's also gotten pretty good at reading Teddy's face despite the handkerchief, but it still takes him by surprise when he notices the wrinkles beside his eyes that give away a covered smile.

"Come on." Teddy's still got him by the hand as he turns and resumes their trek to the creek. "Did your pastor talk to you guys about the big potluck next week? Rabbi Jacobs said it's to strengthen community bonds and be allies across belief. All the churches voted to see if we'd be allowed to go, and even though they voted yes it got Aunt Julie all fired up, but Uncle Darren talked her into going, anyway. He said if we want things to get better, we have to be willing to bend. It'll be cool to get to hang out, don't you think?"

Nash doesn't think much of anything except the way Teddy's fingers are chilled and clammy alongside his all the way to the creek. And how his folks'll probably come down with a sudden illness Sunday morning, necessitating they miss the potluck with *those types*.

At the creek, Teddy pulls his hand free and wads his fingers into fists of jagged, bony knuckles as he hops from foot to foot. "Show me how to punch like you did Chuck that one time and then let's play superheroes."

"Why? So you can punch me?"

"I'll be gentle, promise. If we're going to be allies, we need to be equals, right?"

Nash blinks. "I thought you were talking about faith."

"Well, but it's all the same in principle, right? If I'm going to have your back, then I need to do what you do, so show me."

Nash sighs. He's dodged this one as long as he can, he thinks. Only thing left is to make sure Teddy can hold his own when he inevitably picks a fight while Nash isn't around to squirrel him out of it.

"Well, for firsts, you look stupid with your elbows all the way up by your ears. Haven't you ever seen a fight before?"

Teddy squishes his elbows against his ribs and continues dancing around on the balls of his feet. "No. Have you?"

Seen a fight? No, he supposes he hasn't. But he's picked up the basics, and he knows from practice that swinging from up by your head doesn't work well.

He must take too long to respond because Teddy quits his blusterin' around and goes serious. "He hurts you, doesn't he? I've seen how you are sometimes—all sore and quiet. Quieter than usual, I mean. Is it bad?"

Nash shrugs and looks away. "No," he lies. "It ain't too bad."

"Does he hit Jo too?"

He shakes his head. "I make sure it's just me."

Teddy's eyebrows crush down. "What about your mom?"

"I guess he gets her sometimes too."

"No, I mean, how come she doesn't do something? Shouldn't she be the one who makes sure it's just her? Or nobody at all?"

That's a question Nash has asked himself for a long, long time and he ain't never come up with a good enough answer.

CHAPTER FIVE
The loft

He takes it easy, putting Teddy through the motions of a fight until he doesn't look so awkward hooking his arm through the air. He's still so little he can't do much damage, but at least he won't humiliate himself. Teddy wants to keep practicing, but Nash lies and says he's bored—partly to get out of it and partly to give Teddy a break.

It's not that Teddy doesn't know his limits. The problem is that he'd rather ignore them than heed them, and Nash has only got so many piggyback rides in him. So it's up to him to make sure Teddy doesn't overdo it so bad that he can't make the walk home without heaving up a lung and doing another overnight in the hospital.

They kick around the creek for a little while, then make

believe they have superpowers and rain terror on the enemy
aliens that take the shape of the trees lining the creek, until
the sun settles atop the horizon and threatens to leave them
in the dark.

On the gravel road that connects their homes, they make
plans to do it all again the next day.

"Nash, wait!"

He stops and when he turns, Teddy is right there,
handkerchief down around his neck, and looking up at him
with an unreadable expression.

"Put that back on, would you? If you have an attack, you
won't be allowed out tomorrow."

Teddy tugs at the handkerchief but doesn't lift it back
over his nose. "You want to do this again tomorrow?"

"'Course." He pauses and considers Teddy's anxious
stance for the first time. "Don't you?"

"Yeah. Yeah, I just... So what Jo said didn't bother you?"

Nash blinks at him. "Did Jo say something?"

His sister says a lot of things, most of which he filters out
until she says something that actually matters. Weeks can
pass that way.

"She— On the bus? About— About us?" His cheeks flare
red, but he screws up his mouth and holds Nash's stare like
he dared himself not to look away. "About us kissing and
stuff."

"Oh." Nash recalls her going on about that, but he hadn't
taken her seriously. Looking at Teddy now, he wonders if he
should have. Or if, at the very least, he should have checked
with Teddy sooner to make sure he wasn't. "She was just
messing around."

"Yeah, I know, but did her saying it bother you?"

"Why would it?"

Teddy's embarrassment burns away to a familiar irritation. "I don't know, maybe because lots of people get all weird about guys kissing, and I didn't know if you were one of them."

"Oh. Well, I guess I'm not. Are you?"

"Am I what?"

"Weirded out by guys kissing?"

Teddy clams up, searching Nash's eyes through clear lenses. He takes a breath and pushes it out. Steps back. "No. See you tomorrow."

Nash watches him spin on his heel and strike off down the road with a peculiar twist in his belly. Like Teddy was tryin' to tell him something important, and he just wasn't quick enough to pick it up.

When Nash gets home, the blare of the TV is audible from the porch. He takes in the familiar scream of the wrestling announcer and makes an abrupt turn for the barn.

They don't have much in the way of land—not like Chuck's family who owns all the farmland around both his and Teddy's houses and more besides—but they've got enough to keep a few cattle fat and happy, if only they had the funds. When Daddy's in a sharin' mood, he talks about when he was growin' up here, how it was a proper ranch with a whole herd and that by the time he was Nash's age he was workin' near full time carin' for 'em.

Usually that's when his sharin' mood takes a turn as he remembers he had to sell the herd and near all the land around the time Nash was born and Nash has to make himself scarce to avoid a whoopin' just for being around.

Wrestling nights are like that. Daddy gets all amped up and by the time the match is over, he's sloshed and lookin' for a fight. So, Nash does what's reasonable and stays well away.

He slips into the old barn and takes a moment for his eyes to adjust to the dimness. The heavy scent of old straw warms the air, mingled in with that musky animal smell that ain't cleared even though it's been years since the barn was host to any livestock. Smells like home to him.

There's a shuffling from the loft and then Jo's face is peering down at him.

"Hurry up, I snatched a box of crackers from the kitchen and I don't mind eatin' 'em all without you."

Nash scurries up the ladder, stomach squeezing all empty around the memory of lunch.

"How long you been out here?"

"Not long." She hands him a new sleeve of crackers, then picks a cracker out the top of the open sleeve in her fist. "He just got started, and I figured you'd come out here rather than have to get past him." Her easy company turns hard. "And don't think I'm not gonna get you back for lyin' about Mama wantin' help earlier. I ain't forgot your sins."

"Drama queen." He roughly shoves her head between her knees and ruffles her hair. She can act as tough as she wants, but she'll always be his dumb little sister.

A sharp pinch to his thigh has him flinching away and his crackers get lost in the ensuing scuffle.

He waits until Jo is flat on her back, rattling the rafters with her snores before he slips down the ladder and creeps into the night. It's eerie quiet in the between months before the bugs and birds go loud again. Only the distant scream of a coyote disrupts the stillness.

He steps over the creaky step and slinks onto the porch.

It's quiet inside too. Dark and silent in the way dead things are. He closes the door behind him, gentle like settling a duckling atop a pond, and steps softly through the front room toward the glow of the kitchen.

He's sure if it were Daddy sitting up at the table he'd be makin' his usual racket, but he still waits until he hears a familiar sniffle before he steps into the light.

It's Mama with a fistful of damp tissues and half her face swollen up and pitched a sore pink.

"You alright, Mama?"

She flinches away from his voice like he whipped her, but then she gathers herself and snarls, "Get the hell out."

"He got you?"

"You know damn well he did. You made sure of it, didn't you? Get back to your sister, Nash. You made your choice."

"But, Mama—"

"I said get the hell out!"

He backs out of the room quick. Once she drops her face in her hands, he turns tail and beats a retreat to the barn with his heart smarting. He didn't think he was picking Jo over Mama, but she's right. They left her alone to face Daddy in one of his fits. And he left her again just now, rather than risk her shouting bringing Daddy down on both of them.

He don't sleep much that night. Not with the memories of Mama's tear-stained face lingering with the echo of her voice. Rather than sleep next to Jo in the loft, he slips into the pen underneath and curls up against a spiky pile of straw him and Jo shaped into the likeness of what they imagine to be a dairy cow. If a few tears sneak down his cheeks, then that's between him and Miss Merry May.

He messed up. He doesn't know what he was thinkin'—

Well, that ain't true. He was thinkin' of Mama's bruised face and how she missed a whole two days of work waiting for it to heal up some, and then they couldn't afford to get him a cake for his birthday. He was thinkin' about how alone she is with nobody lookin' out for her.

Anyway, call him a fool because he knew Daddy was gearin' up for a wallopin' kind of night and Nash stood himself right in the center of it and let it hit him.

Teddy won't speak to him. Or maybe he won't speak to Teddy because all Teddy wants to talk about is getting revenge or narcing to his aunt and uncle, and Nash doesn't want any of those things. He wants a break. He wants to not hurt.

He thought if he stayed, then Mama would have stayed. He thought if he showed her he listened and he cares they would turn into a team, into allies, and together they could get Daddy to stop or leave. But when Daddy started in on him, she shut her bedroom door and didn't come out. It hurts almost more than his body. He's been limping for two days now, and his knee looks all sorts of angry in the way Teddy wishes Nash would be, but he can't. He just can't.

CHAPTER SIX
The garage

It's the Saturday after Teddy gets 100 percent on their chapter test that his uncle beckons Nash into the garage.

Nash hesitates, looking for Teddy, but he's in the kitchen putting the dishes from their celebratory supper in the sink and listening intently as Mrs. Spinoza, speaking softly, arranges their Saturday night worship things on the table—a long twisty candle, a fancy cup filled with grape juice, and a small box that makes the whole cupboard it's kept in smell like pumpkin pie.

Loath to interrupt and with no excuse readily available, Nash steps into the garage with his trepidations clutched tight to his chest, ready to sprint back into the house at a moment's notice.

The garage is a one-car stall, and a half-assembled Mustang takes up the majority, while all four tires sit in a stack by the door. He thinks the original color might have been red, but the door facing him is white and the front fender is orange, so it's difficult to say for sure.

Against the back wall, a stained, slanted workbench is littered with parts, tools, bits, and bobs, only a few of which Nash recognizes. The whole place has a stink of chemicals and metal, but Teddy's uncle breathes it in deep and smiles.

He picks up a socket wrench and a flashlight, then hands the flashlight to Nash.

"Hold this for me, would you?"

Unsure what else to do, Nash accepts the flashlight but doesn't step down from the short stairway that leads into the garage.

Teddy's uncle lays down and scoots his upper body under the car. "Right here if you can angle it."

The clang of ringing metal makes Nash jump, then scurry down the stairs to the front bumper. He lifts onto his toes, but he can't see where Teddy's uncle is pointing.

"I can't see." He braces for ridicule or shouting, but Teddy's uncle laughs lightly instead.

"That's what the extra light is for."

His cheeks flush with heat. "I mean, I'm not tall enough."

If the car was on the ground, he'd be able to see inside, no problem, but the stands holding it up to allow Teddy's uncle to fit underneath lift the innards just out of sight.

"Oh, right. There's a stepstool in here somewhere. Check back by the workbench."

Nash finds it, an old plastic thing covered in splotches of white and yellow paint like what's on the walls in the kitchen. "I got it."

He sets it in front of the car, climbs atop it, and clicks on the light. It reflects at him from the shiny silver of the socket wrench.

"Perfect. Hold it right there."

Teddy's uncle gets to work. He also gets to chatting. Nash doesn't say much, but he doesn't need to because Teddy's uncle does all the talking. He's never been this chatty before, but apparently, all he needed was a tool in his hand and something to keep him busy to open up the floodgates.

He doesn't talk about anything overly important, mostly just cars. Sports cars, race cars, the go-cart he wants to build with Teddy someday if he could just convince him to put down the Pokémon cards for five minutes. He talks about trucks that'll last years and trucks that are better left on the side of the road. He talks about his first car, a station wagon. He talks about his high school girlfriend's first car, a Jeep, and how he got it stuck while out mudding and rather than confess to her old man about it, he called up all his friends to help him tow it out. They got three more cars stuck before he finally caved and called on the adults for help. He talks about how long his old man laughed before he lifted a single finger, and how it was so embarrassing he stopped answering his girlfriend's calls, and how after a week of being ignored she finally sent her cousin over to tell him he was dumped.

It's... nice. Nash is almost disappointed when Teddy pokes his head into the garage, wrinkles his nose at the smell, and then barks a laugh upon seeing Nash stood in front of the car holding the flashlight.

"Uncle Darren! Nash is *my* friend." To Nash, he says, "I thought you left."

"He's being kind enough to help me out, since someone

is too busy."

"Better him than me!" Teddy's grin fades and he looks at Nash seriously. "You should get home soon, though. It's getting dark."

Mr. Spinoza slides out from under the car. "I'll drive you."

"I'm fine to walk," Nash says quickly. He clicks off the flashlight and holds it out as Mr. Spinoza gets to his feet. "Honest."

He smiles, but he's making too much eye contact as he says, "I insist. It's the least I can do after you helped me today. Come on, I'll grab my keys."

Nash stays rooted to the spot. He doesn't know what to do. Daddy's gonna flip his lid if some stranger pulls into the drive without him knowin' about it in advance, and the very *last* thing Nash wants is him knowing about it in advance.

Mr. Spinoza stops on the stairs when Teddy, his eyes fixed on Nash with a worried wrinkle between his eyebrows, doesn't move from the doorway.

Mr. Spinoza cocks his head and considers him from the top step. "Or," he says, "I could drop you off at the bottom of the hill if you'd prefer."

Nash's gaze slides past Mr. Spinoza to Teddy. He nods, chin bobbing, as though to urge Nash to accept the compromise.

"Alright," Nash says after a beat. And then after another, "Thank you."

Mr. Spinoza smiles. "It's the least I can do."

Teddy steps back and pushes the door open. "You have to make *Havdalah* with us first."

"Thank you for the reminder," Mr. Spinoza says with just a hint of dryness. He turns to Nash. "Would you like to join us?"

"That's okay," Nash says quickly. He knows the
ceremony is a short one, but he can never understand the
words.

"Here's fine," Nash says as they approach the bottom of the
hill. Twilight is settling rapidly into full night, but it's not yet
so dark that he'll be in trouble for it. Not unless Daddy is
lookin' to pick a fight and, in that case, it won't matter how
early or late he is. "You can turn around in that farm entrance
there."

"Sure." Mr. Spinoza turns into the grassy inlet off the
road and shifts into park.

Nash undoes his seatbelt, but before he can get his door
open, Mr. Spinoza clears his throat.

"Listen, Nash. I was thinking, you're up and around
pretty early most days, right?" He doesn't look at him as he
drums his fingers against the steering wheel and stares off
over the farmland. "And since Teddy takes his day of rest
very seriously, that leaves you a lot of time waiting around
on him."

"Umm..."

"It doesn't have to be every Saturday, but I'm usually up
and working on the car around eight. If you want to stop by
and help out, I'd appreciate the extra hands."

"Oh." Nash blinks several times. "I—"

"If you're in the mood, stop by. I'll leave the door up so
you don't have to knock and wake anybody. Think about it."

Nash frowns. "I thought you guys weren't allowed to do

stuff like that on Saturdays."

Mr. Spinoza's eyes go all twinkly like he's about to tell a joke, or a secret. "Sometimes things that are work for most, are rest for others. God and I have an understanding."

Must be nice. He can't say he'd use a direct line with the almighty to negotiate the definition of rest, but, well, maybe that's why he ain't got one.

He pops open his door. "Thanks for the ride."

Mr. Spinoza smiles, and he seems to mean it when he says, "Anytime."

Nash surprises himself by showing up outside the Spinoza's garage bright and early the following Saturday morning. The summer sun is hot on his neck as he treks up the hill. The door is open as Mr. Spinoza said it would be and an old rock song about sparkling earrings and brown skin is playing just loud enough to carry to the end of the drive.

When Nash approaches, Mr. Spinoza holds out a socket wrench with a smile. They don't speak except about the engine they're trying to put back together, by which he means Mr. Spinoza talks almost nonstop about how all the parts fit together and what they do and how to tell when somethin's off. After an hour, it's the easiest Nash has ever felt in an adult's presence.

When he comes back the following Saturday, the door is open, the same radio station is playing, and a shiny red toolbox is waiting for him by the car's front bumper.

CHAPTER SEVEN

The wrong thing

Teddy doesn't care much for fixin' up cars—too smelly and dirty—but Nash learns that if you give him a computer, he can tear the thing apart and put it back together within a weekend. Unfortunately, his uncle don't know a damn thing about computers and Teddy ain't interested in turning teacher.

That's what Aunt Julie says anyhow when she's explaining to Nash over a sink of soap suds why Uncle Darren has taken a liking to him. It don't clear up nothin', but then again, he gave up trying to understand why adults do what they do a long time ago. He's just pleased to have his very own set of tools that he gets to take home and do what he wants with so long as he keeps 'em clean and remembers to bring 'em with him every Saturday.

He thinks back on what Aunt Julie told him over the dishes when Uncle Darren takes him and Teddy out back with a plastic sack full of empty Coke cans and a shotgun.

Uncle Darren says every man ought to know his way around a gun. It's how to protect yourself, and how to keep your family fed for a whole winter, assuming you've got the freezer space. It's what he says, but Nash thinks on what Aunt Julie told him as she wiped down the breakfast plates and he wonders if that's truly the whole of why they're out here.

Even so, Uncle Darren's words have an effect on him. Protection and survival. He can understand protection and survival.

Teddy, though, seems to be suffering the opposite effect judging by the pinched set to his mouth and the low V of his brow. He don't seem to be likin' this lesson one bit better than he liked any of the engine stuff that Uncle Darren says Nash has a knack for.

Uncle Darren sees it too because he stops setting the cans on the fence and says, "I know what you're thinking, Ted, but your parents might have lived if they'd had a way to protect themselves. I want better for you."

It's the wrong thing to say.

Teddy puffs up like blowfish and his face turns all red 'n' splotchy. Through snapping teeth, he spits, "They'd have lived if some asshole with a gun hadn't killed them."

Oh.

Neither Uncle Darren nor Nash try to stop him from stalking back to the house, all stiff with jerking limbs. The door slams and Uncle Darren sighs and starts packing the Coke cans back into the sack.

Nash clears his throat. "Mr. Spinoza, I'd still like to learn. If you're willin', I mean."

He pauses and looks Nash over. Then he looks up at the house with an unhappy set to his mouth and sighs. "I suppose you would."

Nash doesn't know what he means by that, if he's thinking he's the violent type or something worse, so he hurries to explain. "I'd like to know how to protect myself. I — I just want to be safe."

Uncle Darren turns his attention back to him with a look like Nash broke his heart. After a beat, he repeats, "I suppose you would." He tips the last of the cans into the sack. "You up for a little drive? Teddy won't want to hear us banging around out here."

Nash hesitates at the thought of leaving the property. Technically, he's not supposed to leave his own property despite bein' over the hill at Teddy's more often than not. If he gets caught, he'll be in a world of trouble. Then again, when ain't he in trouble?

"Where to?"

Teddy doesn't talk to him for an entire week after that, which, knowin' Teddy, is mighty worrisome. Nash is expectin' a blow up, a fight, something, anything. Teddy's never quiet unless he doesn't have air to make the words go. Even the teachers notice he's actin' all strange, and somehow Nash ends up having a chat with the school counselor over it.

He keeps his mouth shut about what sparked their

disagreement, no matter how sweet she wheedles for the truth of it. Him and Teddy have been something like best friends for years and that day in his backyard was the first time Teddy ever mentioned what happened to his parents. He knows better than to spread it around, even if Teddy's avoiding him.

So he's surprised when Friday fizzles to a close and Teddy sits beside him on the bus like everything's normal.

"Wanna go to the creek?"

Nash stares at him. He's got his usual handkerchief around his neck, ready to tug up over his nose once the bus stops in the dusty patch of road between their houses, and he's staring straight ahead at the initials scratched into the seat in front of them.

It's not the right time of year for it, but Teddy asked and it's the first thing he's said to him since Sunday. Of course, he says yes.

For once, Jo is easy to shake. She's been buggin' him all week about why him and Teddy haven't been sitting together on the bus, and it's painful obvious that they're not through their issue yet just lookin' at how still and silent they are for the drive.

She departs toward home with a significant look that tells him she'll be harassing him for the details the second he gets back.

That leaves the two of them. Teddy tightens his handkerchief around the back of his head, tucks the bottom into his T-shirt, and then sets off without a backward glance. Nash trails after.

They trek through the field—soybeans this year. They're lush and green after the long, hot summer, but Teddy's brisk walk doesn't leave time for marveling at the wonder of them, and Nash knows better than to test the limit right now. He dogs his heels all the way to the creek, across the felled tree, and to the little clearing with the roughed up trees they've been awful unkind to over the years with their roughhousing.

Teddy spins around to face him and Nash teeters to a stop, half a step from bowling him over.

"Let's spar," Teddy says. His glasses are fogged, but his shoulders are thrown back and he's looking Nash in the eye.

His stomach drops. He's quiet as he says, "If you wanna hit me, just hit me."

Teddy rips his handkerchief down. "This isn't about hurting— I don't want to hurt you, stupid." The fog on his lenses is slow to clear. "You went with Uncle Darren, and he taught you his way of protection. Well, this is mine." He gestures at the clearing around them. "If you can learn from him, then you can learn from me too."

"I'm sorry, I—"

"I know why you did it. I don't like it, but I know, okay? If you think you need that, then you need this too. Let's just… Let's just spar."

The fog finally fades and reveals Teddy's eyes. He expected anger. He's so used to anger. Instead, there's something desperate in Teddy's stare. Something pleading and grasping and earnest.

Nash breathes out and flicks a glance at Teddy's backpack. "You got your inhaler?"

Teddy nods and swings his bag under his arm to root around in it. Once he finds the inhaler, he brings it to his lips, then pauses. "We're gonna spar?"

Nash shakes his head. "When have I ever turned you down? 'Course we are."

He must not've been expecting that answer because Teddy stares at him over the inhaler, searching for something. Nash wouldn't know what for. It's the truth. The only thing he ever denies him is the spot at the top of the class and that's only when he can keep ahead of him, which ain't always.

"What?"

Teddy shrugs and finally drops his gaze as he sucks in a lungful of whatever it is they put in those things that lets him breathe. He holds it as he stows away his inhaler, yanks his zipper shut, and tosses his bag at the base of a tree.

Nash puts his beside it as Teddy releases his breath and fixes his handkerchief back around his head.

"Pin or first down?"

"Pin," Nash says after thinking on it.

The only real difference is how much scrabbling around in the dirt they do, as opposed to him getting jabbed at with sharp fists and bony knees. And maybe... Maybe it's been a while since he was close with someone.

Nash is sore by the time they're done, and Teddy's face is pink but his breathing sounds alright, if heavy. They're side by side, flat on their backs, watching the sky dim through thick leaves overhead, milking the last few minutes before Teddy has to hurry home. Nash uses the time to revel in the comfort of the heat against his side after so long spent awkward and distant, and to embrace the relief that comes at the end of summer.

It's not that he minds the heat. Summer means a lot of

things, but mostly summer means Teddy is stuck inside, which ain't so bad during the day when all the adults are at work and it's just them, but summer also means no school-provided lunch. It means bein' home more than he's not. It means ain't nobody need to see him so Daddy can mark him up as much as he wants—so long as he's fit to sit in a pew come Sunday morning.

But that's behind him now, and this year him and Teddy are in the same class, which always makes for a good year. Means he can keep him out of trouble easier, but also they get to see each other every day and sit together at lunch so long as Teddy's finished avoiding him.

He tips his head to the side. Teddy's got his glasses held loosely on his belly so Nash can see from the bridge of his nose to the sweat soaking the roots of his hair without impediment.

Teddy tips his head and meets his stare, all brown-eyed and sweet-faced like he rarely is. So that's why Nash says what he's been wanting to say all week.

"I'm sorry about your mom and dad. And I'm sorry I—"

"Don't." Teddy turns back to the sky and Nash can tell by the furrow of his brow that there's a frown behind his handkerchief. "Just... don't."

Nash licks his lips but swallows back the next apology that swells onto his tongue. Teddy doesn't want to hear it, but one way or another, he needs to say it. So he keeps his mouth shut, eyes on the trees, and finds the hand holding Teddy's glasses.

There's only a moment of resistance before Teddy releases his hold and allows Nash to twist their fingers together. He can feel his eyes on him now, but he doesn't turn and look. If he doesn't look, then Teddy's expression can't shame him into pulling away. His heart is beating curiously strong, but he doesn't let go.

He half-expects Teddy to shake him off and call him queer. He thinks maybe if they were anywhere but here, that would be a reasonable reaction. But here... The creek is the only place in the whole cussing town that's safe.

Teddy must know it too because after he's looked his fill, he turns his face back to the trees and squeezes.

CHAPTER EIGHT

The world tips

So long as he keeps sparring whenever they get the chance, Teddy doesn't give him grief about guns or his dad, even though Uncle Darren takes Nash out twice more to practice shooting. He does okay. It don't come as easy as numbers or engines but it comes. It comes well enough that Uncle Darren starts dreaming up hunting trips that Nash won't never be able to go on with his daddy around.

Uncle Darren must be talking about it at home too, because after Nash improves some, Aunt Julie sits him down for a long talk at the kitchen table. She tells him about responsibility and the difference between protecting property and protecting life, and that one of those might be worth killin' for, but the other definitely ain't. She tells him about growing up in Arizona on a ranch with her big, loud family, and the necessity of keepin' the herd safe from coyotes and other critters. But she also tells him about the terrible accidents that followed forgetting, even for only a moment, that guns kill.

It freaks him out some. He ain't ever thought of killin' anybody, just keeping him and his safe and fed, but she sets him to thinkin' about it. It's several weeks before he agrees to go out with Uncle Darren again.

Teddy knows he's still going, but they don't talk about it, not directly. Nash knows it eats at him and he knows it'll boil over eventually, but he expects when it happens for the target to be him. Not Chuck.

It's recess and the usual crowd is hassling him and Teddy on the blacktop when Teddy takes his newfound skill and plants it knuckles-first in Chuck's face.

For a moment, Nash is just as dumbstruck as everyone else. Little Teddy, not even of a height to tickle the underside of Chuck's chin, decks him clean in the mouth. There's blood and shouting, and about the time Chuck's buddies menace forward, Nash gets over his shock and puts his back to Teddy's.

It's their first time not fighting each other, and he expects to get smeared, but luckily it seems to be the other five's first fight period. All-in-all, they make it out the other side in decent shape. Teddy is grinning like a shark, eyebrow busted open and oozing as the teacher on recess duty scolds them all the way to the principal's office.

Nash can't quite believe it. Can't believe they managed to scrape their way free without getting their teeth knocked out and their guts kicked in. Can't stop looking at the way Teddy is grinning like he just took on the world and won.

They get in awful trouble, of course, considering Teddy threw the first punch. Part of him wants to argue that he doesn't deserve equal punishment, but he just calls Mama at the diner and lets her know he needs picked up and brought home on account of bein' suspended for a week.

He imagines he'll be sore about it later, but Teddy is still grinning and the stunning absence of his regret is infectious. It buoys him right 'till the door swings open and his daddy steps in.

All the air sucks clean out of the room outside the principal's office where Nash and Teddy are sitting side by side in matching plastic chairs. Then Daddy's eyes light upon him and Nash goes cold all over.

And Teddy—Teddy, who looks from Nash to his daddy and knows who he is, but don't ever know when to keep his mouth shut—says, "Nice to finally meet you, Mr. Owens. Nash isn't in trouble, right? He was only doing what you taught him, after all."

All Nash can do is sit with ice-water sweat puckered all up and down his back while Teddy glares Daddy right in his eyes and Daddy stares back like he ain't never seen a boy quite like Theodore Spinoza. Of course he hasn't. Boys like Teddy ain't long for this world on account of being so goddamn stupid, and neither is any boy fool enough to tie himself to one—knowin' better all while fitting his feet directly in the sunken dirt impressions left in Teddy's wake.

Daddy's stare flickers from Teddy to instead drill into Nash all sun-fire and heat-stroke. "You been tellin' tall tales, son?"

"No, sir."

He hates himself for the warble that betrays his fear and

draws Teddy's stare from Daddy, stopped still in the doorway, to Nash's shivering self.

"No?" To the secretary, Daddy flashes a smile like a badge, one that says he's the authority here and ain't these kids funny for thinkin' they're smarter 'n him.

She smiles stiffly back and collects a stack of paper before stepping into the copy room and closing the door.

Daddy swivels back around. "Did you tell me 'No,' boy? You think there's truth in an accusation like that?"

His breathing quickens. Teddy is staring at him like he's never seen him before and he hates, he *hates* that Teddy's seein' him like this, but Daddy's lookin' at him like he's doing all the right things to justify getting his bones all broken up and handed back in a sack at the bottom of the lake, so there's nothin' he can do but tremble and try to say the words Daddy's lookin' to hear.

"No, sir."

Daddy's face goes all flushed and panic buzzes in Nash's ears like a thousand bug zappers. He can't think for all the noise. His lungs are all stopped up, too full to get the air he needs, and *Lord*, but it's hard to think. The magic words exist, but he can't figure 'em out in time to keep Teddy from opening his mouth and signing his death certificate.

Never met a bully too big or a fight too petty to pick, Teddy balls up his bony fists, steps in front of Nash, and says, "He didn't tell me anything. I've seen for myself what you do to him and if you hurt him again, my uncle's gonna call the cops! He promised he would!"

Daddy looks surprised for a moment. Then he laughs. "You don't know what you've seen, little boy. My boy plays rough." He jerks his chin. "C'mon Nash. We ought to get home so I can figure out what to do with you."

Through numb lips, Nash says, "The principal was wantin' to talk to—"

Daddy shoots him a look so sharp he feels the cut reverberate through his bones. He near swallows his tongue in his hurry to shut up.

"Did I or did I not tell you to do somethin'? Get in the goddamn truck, Nash Owens."

"Yes, sir." His legs barely hold him as he stands. He pinches Teddy hard as he goes past, silently begging him to keep quiet. Then he follows Daddy out the door and doesn't look back.

He flinches at the sharp snap of the door closing, rattling the pictures and windows in their frames. For a moment, he considers making a run for it. He considers bolting out the back. He considers—for a flash, for an *instant*—the gun he knows is just up the hill.

But Aunt Julie was clear, and Daddy's never killed him before, so he ain't likely to do so now. Besides, it's always worse when he tries to protect himself.

That's what he tells himself anyway, but it's hard to imagine anything worse than the fury boiling off Daddy as he looms over him in the hollow heart of the family room.

He unbuckles his belt. "You know what's comin', don't you boy?"

Nash's knees are quaking so hard, he couldn't run now if he wanted.

"Yes, sir," he gasps.

Daddy's belt whips free of the loops, and he takes hold of

the end opposite the buckle.

Nash's breathing is coming in nothin' but gasps now. Head swimming in terror, it's all he can do to keep his feet under him and his bowels inside.

"Today's lesson," Daddy says, all purposeful and slow, "is to be mindful of the company you keep. You'll find yourself payin' for your friends' missteps just as surely as you do your own, and God help you if they rub off on you."

His first swing cuts across Nash's cheek. The biting shock of it is enough to clear his head into remembering that he's suspended and won't nobody be seein' him for an entire week.

It's then that he realizes exactly how much trouble he's in.

The first thing he hears when he comes to is crying. Everything hurts so bad, he assumes it's him until the snorting, snotty hiccup reveals itself to be comin' from Jo.

He tries to comfort her. *It's okay Joey. Go wait for me in the loft. I'll get you when it's all over.*

He can't hardly breathe to get the words out. In all the riot of pain swallowing over him, he can't locate his tongue.

It's never been this bad before.

Something sharp like fire pierces his chest, and he cries out, more a whimper than a shout. He curls up to protect himself, but moving only makes everything worse until he's spinning and even the floor holding him up feels distant.

"It's okay, it's okay. Uncle Darren's coming. You're gonna be okay."

That's Teddy's voice, but he shouldn't be here. That'll only set Daddy off all over again and then... Well, he'd take it out on Nash like usual, but he doesn't think there's any more he could take so maybe he'd just go for Teddy directly, or even Jo.

He fights to open his eyes, to tell Teddy to get out, to run, to hide, anything. Anything but be here for Daddy to find. But his eyelids are so puffy and thick, try as he might, he can't open them, can't see. He can't move his arm neither, and his leg and hip burn like fire every time he so much as twitches.

Now the crying is coming from him, crawling out of his chest in great heaves, and it *hurts*. Oh God, it hurts. He's never been strong enough to stop Daddy, but he could at least stand between him and Jo. Now he can't even stand. He can't even open his eyes.

Jo is closer now. He thinks that's her, dripping on his face and patting his hair, but Teddy is there too, rambling about hospital and help and his uncle.

The door bangs open.

Fear chokes him in a sudden dizzy rush. With a wordless cry, he lurches at where Jo is sobbing and Teddy is chattering and knocks into someone, maybe both of them, but then it's Uncle Darren's low, steady voice comin' closer, not Daddy's rumbling fury.

Things get muddy.

Moving was a bad idea. His head's swimmin' so bad from the pain that what's happening around him seems to blink in and out. Someone's speaking soothing and calm while another voice spits out an anxious flurry of words and Jo hiccups.

New voices, ones he doesn't recognize, ask questions he

can't understand as they move and shift him around until all
he can do is sob while someone, Jo, he thinks, pats his hair.

A pair of lips meet his forehead and he thinks it's Jo until
Teddy whispers against his skin, "I'm gonna fix this. I swear
I'll make it right. I swear."

Then the world tips like he's falling into the sky and he
doesn't remember much anything after that.

Of the following week, he carries out of it two memories:

1. Jo and Teddy sacked out at his bedside in hard plastic
chairs in a beige room, all falling into each other and
drooling.

2. The hard look Mama gave him when he first seen her,
still in her apron from the diner, smelling like frying oil
and maple syrup. There was no concern in it. No
apology for sending Daddy to the school in her place.
Just a look like Nash let her down.

Nobody sees Daddy again. Considering he emptied their
savings and cleared his half of the closet, they don't expect
he'll ever be comin' back, even though Mama told the cops
that she'd be pressin' no charges on account of havin' no
word on the truth of things 'cept that of a little boy who's just
been suspended for fighting.

That's a third memory, he supposes, 'cuz two years go by
and he ain't never forgot how those officers closed up their
notepads and trooped out of the room without a single

glance at him laid up in the hospital bed, unable to move.

CHAPTER NINE
His perfect day

It's one of those in-between days that occurs between winter and spring—one of those special days when Teddy can play outside without the outside trying to do him in. Nash is taking full advantage with a game of kickball, even though his hip is throbbing and Jo is relentless in her mockery of the strange way he runs. Like a hobbling skip, she says. Like an old hobo who found the winning lottery ticket in the trash.

His only comfort is in Teddy's assurance that he doesn't look half as silly as Jo does aping after him.

Regardless, after all this hoppin' about, tomorrow is bound to be a cane day. He don't mind though, not really. It's worth it.

"Tag him, Teddy, you soft-headed idiot!"

"I'm *trying!*"

Nash's foot tangles in Jo's-sweater-turned-home-plate a second before the kickball shoves between his shoulder blades with what feels like all of Teddy's weight behind it. He topples and Teddy goes down with him in a tangle of limbs and breathless cursing.

He sucks in a mouthful of dirt and succumbs to a coughing fit made difficult by his winded state and Teddy sprawled on his back. He throws an elbow at him, and Teddy rolls off to land face up at his side with a dazed expression.

He catches Nash's eye. "Okay?" he pants.

Nash turns away to avoid hacking and spewing mud in his friend's face. "Fine," he chokes, then spits in the dirt and pushes himself up onto his knees. His right hip screams abuse, so he ends up on his ass instead of his feet. Then he exhales long and slow as he stretches out his leg.

Teddy rocks upright and pulls his shirt over his nose, only to make a face and release it. "Place your bets. What's going to set off my asthma first, the dirt we kicked up or my B.O.?"

"B.O.," he and Jo chant in unison.

She plops down beside them with the ball in her lap, round cheeks flushed red and sweat dotting her forehead. "I'm not lookin' forward to sitting next to you two smelly heaps at the parlor."

"The parlor?" Nash echoes. "Nobody's goin' to the parlor. I was safe."

"Bullshit!" Teddy stabs a finger at him. "I tagged you! You were out!"

"I touched base first."

Teddy stabs his finger at Jo next. "Jo saw it! Back me up."

"I already said, didn't I?"

She throws the ball at Teddy's head and Nash rolls his eyes as the pair squabble in the dirt. It's no use arguing when they gang up on him. To Jo, he says, "You're filching the car keys this time."

The ice cream parlor in Buford Hills is cramped, sticky, and perfect. Nobody questions what Nash is doing driving Mama's old beat-up sedan because nobody knows them and nobody much cares to. So long as they don't cause a ruckus and they're careful to park the car off the main road, where nobody sees three gangly not-quite-teenagers clamber out of it, they can go wherever they want.

It's the most freedom he's ever had, and he's not sure he can give it up now that he's had a taste of it.

"You're getting the same old butter pecan?" Teddy complains. He has a noxious green monstrosity in his fist that's already melting a rivulet over his knuckles.

Nash shoves an extra napkin at him. "I know what I like."

Jo snorts and saws off the end of her banana with her spoon. "Sure, you do."

Teddy eyeballs her sundae with deep suspicion and scoots even further against Nash's side to steer clear of the thing. Nash switches his cone to his left hand lest Teddy jostle it to the floor.

"What's that supposed to mean?"

She scoops up whipped cream and chocolate sauce along with her banana and states, "You're more blind to what you like than a baby bat what was born wrong."

He glances at Teddy, who's too busy racing the melting of his ice cream while keeping the banana in his line of sight to offer commentary.

"Whatever that means."

She pops her spoon in her mouth then says through her food, "Means you're stupid, but I ain't gettin' involved. You can figure it out your own self."

He rolls his eyes at her cryptic commentary and doesn't bother with another follow-up question. Life ain't exactly perfect, but he's happy with what he's got. Mama's out more often nowadays, whether at the diner or the bar, he couldn't say. Jo is as annoying and clingy as ever, and Teddy is the same bullheaded, loud-mouth he's always been—but Nash can't complain. It's a beautiful spring day, and he's eating ice cream with his favorite people. What kind of fool would he be to start pickin' at things best left alone?

Teddy finishes sucking his knuckle clean, then asks, "Are we still talking about ice cream?"

Teddy and Jo are squabbling over the radio when Nash turns into the driveway and spots the Spinozas' car parked in Mama's usual spot.

"Both'a you, hush up."

In the passenger seat, Teddy turns to face the front, then hisses out a curse as he notices the car. The last few months, he's been getting real comfortable with the swears, but never where Uncle Darren and Aunt Julie might hear.

Jo squishes up between the seats as Nash reluctantly

parks alongside it in the wide circle of dirt they call a driveway. "Think they're lookin' for Teddy?"

"Why else would they be here? Askin' after Merry May?"

Jo flicks his ear hard, then falls back before he can pop her nose like he wants.

Teddy passes Nash his cane. "What do we do?"

"Jo, you go in first."

"Me? Why me?"

"You're the best liar we got. You can kick up a big stink about how me and Teddy were leavin' you out again and so you stormed off in a huff and left us at the creek."

"What if they ask about why the car was gone?"

"Play dumb. Just say you were pretty sure it was there when you came in."

She presses her lips together. "That won't fool 'em if they're all steamed up."

"Then hope they ain't, 'cuz it's the best story we've got."

"You owe me big for this."

"I don't owe you nothin'. You're in the same hot water as us." He ignores the bark of his sore hip and twists around to see her better. "You got ice cream on your chin. Hold still."

He licks his thumb, but before he can remove his thumb from his tongue, she's already wiggling away and shrieking.

"You keep your spit-slicked appendages offa me, Nashery Owens!"

Nash and Teddy hiss in unison.

"Be quiet!"

"Shut up! You're gonna bring the whole town to see what the fuss is about!"

She lowers her voice but maintains her affronted glare. "I can clean up my own self."

Nash gestures at the rearview mirror. "Get on with it,

then."

She makes quick work of cleaning her face and tousles up her hair some, even though it's already all wind-tangled, then she slips out of the car and leaves the door open at Teddy's urging.

It takes some grunting and pushing to get the doors to click shut without the wind-up, but they manage it without making too much racket.

"Save our skins, Jo," Teddy tells her. He reaches to ruffle her hair, but she ducks.

"I still think y'all owe me since I'm the one doin' the savin'."

"And I maintain you don't get a special favor for savin' yourself."

Her eyebrows rise, and she glances from the car to Nash. "I don't have to go with your story, you know. It's not like anybody'd expect *me* to go joy ridin'. I can stroll in with a tale of my simple, peaceful day at the pond and leave you up shit creek."

"You've got some devil in you, Josephine Owens."

She smiles, pretty and cherub cheeked. "Don't we all?"

He and Teddy make it to the creek without incident, despite the way his cane rolls over the hard knobbles and sinks into the soft divots until his wrist and shoulder are near as sore as his hip. Halfway there he wonders if there's a point in going the rest of the way knowin' Jo'll be sent right out after them, but he says nothing, and they finish their walk with Teddy's usual chatter taking up all the air space.

"All I'm saying is, *if* she betrays us, I've got a flash drive and all you'll have to do is plug it into her computer and—"

"You know we ain't got a computer, right?"

"You— Oh yeah. Well, then we can fill her bed with popcorn or something."

"She hardly ever sleeps in her bed."

"What? Where does she sleep?"

Nash averts his eyes and shrugs. He knows it's weird that they still share a bed at their age, but they slept side by side for so many years now neither of them can stand the quiet or the cold. It's one of many ways Daddy's ghost lingers on.

The creek is barely a trickle this year, but they still climb over it and perch atop the fallen tree that connects one shore to the other. Before climbing up, Nash toes out of his boots and leaves his socks balled up beside his cane on a wide, flat rock. He wiggles his toes, savoring the refreshing breeze and the last minutes of peace. Beside him, Teddy keeps his sneakers on and tugs his laces tighter before kicking his legs in the open air over the piddly little stream.

Whatever happens next is sure to put a damper on his perfect day. Even if they get away with taking the car, Uncle Darren or Aunt Julie or both wouldn't stop over unless it was to impart to Mama some disturbance they caused or to collect Teddy.

So he shuts the impending end out of his mind and sets himself to cataloging the cool air between his toes, the familiar bark under his backside that gets smoother every year, and Teddy's energetic babbling, forever barring him from enjoying the peaceful quiet of the woods.

"How's the bike?"

Nash pulls himself from his thoughts at the direct

question. He shrugs. "The same. Haven't touched it much. I'm hanging onto it for a summer project." He meets Teddy's stare through fogged lenses and nods at his handkerchief. "Only got a few days 'till you're not fit to be out of doors, so might as well take my time."

"You don't have to wait because of me."

Nash shakes his head and looks out over the creek. "Her first ride is gonna be goin' up that mountain, and you're comin' with. That's the whole point."

He found the old dirt bike abandoned at the scrapyard he frequents a few times a month, looking to collect anything that might prove useful or fun to tinker with. He's there regular enough that Bonnie knows to call him if anything interesting gets dropped off. She didn't call about the bike, though. He found it by pure luck.

Not being able to show Teddy the view from the mountain that looms over their properties has been a stick in his craw for years, but with the bike, Nash can get him there despite the asthma and his no longer being able to hike it. Only things he'll need to work around are Teddy's allergies and the condition of the thing.

The old girl's engine is seized, so it's some significant work that needs doin' before she'll run, let alone be up for the climb, but he enjoys a challenge and it's not like he's short on time. It only means that the first trip up the mountain will be all the sweeter for the work it'll take to get there.

He clocks the unusual quiet before he registers the weight of Teddy's stare on him. When he does, he turns and meets it.

Teddy's glasses are in his hand, leaving no obstruction to muddy the intensity in his eyes.

"What?" Nash swipes a hand over his cheeks in search of

ice cream even though Teddy is looking him steadfast in the eye.

The move catches Teddy's attention and the next thing Nash knows, Teddy is brushing his knuckles down his cheek with a gentleness that runs contrary to everything he knows Teddy to be.

He don't mean anything by it. It's a friendly thing—a Teddy thing, but shoot if it doesn't stop his heart in its tracks, bein' touched all sweet and tender like that. He thinks the majority of the problem stems from not getting enough hugs as a kid, but he can't deny that there's somethin' about it being *Teddy's* hand on his cheek that makes his stomach go all funny.

Teddy's knuckles linger on his chin as he looks up and meets Nash's stare.

The world stops. The wind dies; the little bit of creek trickling below them dries; and all that's left is the wild thunder between Nash's ears, the tree bark against his palms, and Teddy.

Teddy's thumb brushes his chin as he drops his hand. Then he faces out over the creek with a knot jumping in his jaw.

Nash digs his fingers into tree bark until something pricks under his fingernail and the small spike of pain jolts him back to himself.

He clears his throat and ducks his chin. "Did you get it?"

Teddy doesn't look at him. "Get what?"

Nash raises a hand to wipe his chin, then thinks better of it. "The ice cream."

Now, Teddy looks. He meets Nash's gaze with a furrow to his brow like he did that time Nash was so sick he got every equation on their quiz wrong because the numbers kept wandering around on him. There's a tightness around his eyes that he doesn't recognize. Concern maybe. Worry.

After a long beat, Teddy finally says, "Yeah. I got it."

He's lying, but Nash can't call him on it. He can't work his tongue free from the roof of his mouth, and even if he could he doesn't think he could get any words out past the sudden swelling of his Adam's apple.

Unlike Teddy, he's all too aware of the cruelties people in this world can dish out. He had to learn early how fragile it all is. How easy it would be for someone bigger and meaner to snuff him out. So he doesn't call out the lie, because he doesn't know what will happen if he insists Teddy speak the truth right now. He doesn't know what will change or if he's ready to fight for it. All he knows is he's never been strong enough to stay away when he should, and so it's best that he doesn't look too close at the source of the butterflies tickling his innards.

It's on accident when he puts his hand down and finds Teddy's already there, but when Teddy's breath catches and he doesn't pull away, it's on purpose that he links their pinkies.

Jo arrives not five minutes later, red-cheeked and winded.

"Did y'all have to come all the way out here knowin' I'd have to chase you down?" She doesn't pause for their response. "C'mon. Looked like they were gearin' up for an intervention."

CHAPTER TEN

Beautiful and good

The part that worries Nash the most is that no one cares about the car. Maybe they didn't notice it was gone, or maybe whatever put such dour expressions on Uncle Darren and Aunt Julie's faces is a far bigger problem than a simple joyride.

Also worrying is the way Mama's glittering eyes stick on him like she's anticipating a long-awaited comeuppance.

Him, Teddy, and Jo are lined up on the couch while Mama occupies the recliner in the corner, and Teddy's aunt and uncle stand awkwardly in front of the television.

Uncle Darren clasps his hands and speaks over their heads. "We've been trying for a while to provide Teddy with more of a challenge academically. We've been told 'No' to everything from skipping a grade to developing an accelerated curriculum, so we turned our search beyond Deliverance."

Teddy stiffens against Nash's side. "That test you had me take during winter break. What was that for?"

Uncle Darren fails to hitch up a smile. "It was a placement test for Nonpareil Technical School. You were accepted on a full scholarship."

"Where?"

Teddy talks over Nash. "Can Nash take it too? He'll pass, I know he will."

Aunt Julie shakes her head and keeps her eyes downcast.

Carefully, Uncle Darren says, "Nash can't go."

"Why not?"

"Where?" Nash repeats louder. Teddy's aunt and uncle look at him. "Where's the school?"

His stomach fills with lead as Uncle Darren meets his eyes with heartbreak on his face, but it's Aunt Julie who finally answers him, soft and full of apology.

"North Carolina. On the coast."

Nash rocks back like he's been dealt a blow. Everything goes distant.

North Carolina? Why were they looking so far away? Surely there are decent schools in Tennessee? Unless Tennessee is part of the problem. Unless this is about more than getting away from a subpar school district.

Teddy is on his feet, hands in fists, staring down disapproving Uncle Darren and resigned-but-firm Aunt Julie. Beyond them, Mama sits with a small curl to her lips, like a cat with a bug under its paw.

"I won't go," Teddy declares. "You can't make me."

"Yes, we can," Aunt Julie tells him. "Please don't waste what time you have left being argumentative and bitter."

"You're leaving?" Nash hates how small he sounds. How brittle. And in front of Mama, no less.

Aunt Julie softens. "In August. I'm sorry, Nash. Truly sorry."

He shakes his head, breathing hard.

"Nash—"

He pushes to his feet. He's on the verge of crumbling; he can feel it in his chest. Not here. Not with Mama smirking at him across the room, Jo sitting all quiet 'n' watchful, and Teddy ready to fight the whole world.

He crashes through the front door with a storm wind on his heels. He knows it's Teddy without looking. Knows it like he knows his name. Like he knows something beautiful and good and *his* is being ripped from his hands.

He doesn't make it to the barn before a divot catches the foot of his bad leg and lands him hard on his knees.

Teddy collapses beside him. "Are you alright?"

"No," Nash chokes through the pain. "You're leaving, how could I be—" A heaving breath swallows his words as the first tear breaks free. He knocks it away. "You're *leaving*."

"I won't," Teddy says furiously. "They can't make me. I'll —"

"Would you shut up? Stop pretending like you get a say! Can't you see they've got their minds made up? They probably already got a house and new jobs all lined up, and they're taking you along whether you like it or not."

"So you're just giving up? You're not even going to try to —"

Nash laughs. This is quintessential Teddy. Always thinking he's bigger than he is. Always thinking if he just tries hard enough, he can bend the world to his will.

"When are you gonna figure out that nobody gives a

damn what we want? They only care about makin' sure we fall in line and keep quiet and keep out of the way."

He staggers to his feet and limps the rest of the way to the barn.

"We have until August to change their minds," Teddy says to his back. "We can—"

"We *can't*," Nash spits. "There's nothin' we can do 'cept what we're told." He tears open the door. "Don't follow me. You know what the straw does to you."

He closes the door on Teddy's confusion and anger and limps into Miss Merry May's stall. She's a sorry sight after all these years—half rotted and sighing to pieces with only Jo doing any maintenance to keep her in good form—but he's in no condition to care.

He settles against the familiar hulk of her and waits for the tears that threatened to spill before to return. In the fading light, his head tucked against what a faded blue ribbon denotes as Miss Merry May's neck, a deep hollow ache blooms like a bruise in the core of him. He waits and waits for the world to end, but it doesn't. Night creeps in, the crickets chirp their sawing tune, and his heart continues to beat, aching and injured though it is.

Jo finds him in the morning with a plate of hot eggs. They share it and he makes sure Jo doesn't notice how little of it he eats while she's distracted shoring up Merry May's wandering hindquarters.

When she's satisfied with the shape of her, together, they settle back against Merry's warm flank and watch the dust

motes swirl through the golden sunlight shafts overhead. Jo
blows long and slow and sets them all a-swirling like a
shaken snow globe.

"He waited for you, you know," she says after a fair
while. "Had a fantastic shouting match with Mr. and Mrs.
Spinoza. They left, but he waited 'till Mama got tired of his
lingerin' on and sent him home after dark."

Nash sniffs. "Surprised he didn't come bangin' in after
me."

"He wanted to. I talked him out of it."

"How come?"

She shrugs and picks at a bit of straw. "Thought you
might like to get your head straight without him shoutin' and
stompin' how he does."

"How'd you talk him out of it?"

"Wasn't hard. Must've been somethin' you said to him
more than me." She shoots him a pointed look.

He frowns, recalling how he lost his temper with Teddy.
It ain't somethin' he likes about himself and usually he's
better about smothering it down until it snuffs out.
Yesterday, in all his shock and grief, it got the better of him,
and Teddy paid for it.

"I should apologize."

Jo peers at him curiously. "What'd you say?"

"Nothin' that ain't true, but still."

He sighs, then gets to his feet with a suppressed grunt.
His right side is all stiffness and fire. The walk up to the
house to relieve his bladder is going to be hard enough,
never mind getting all the way up the hill to Teddy's. He
resolves himself to it anyway. They don't have much time. A
handful of months. He's not gonna waste it sulking and
stewing.

"Here." Jo hands him his cane and collects their breakfast plate. "You need me for anything?"

He shakes his head. From here on out, he's on his own. He best get used to it.

Teddy is waiting on the front porch when he's done in the bathroom.

Nash pauses in the doorway, startled to see him, and it's all the opportunity Teddy needs to latch onto him in a quick and bruising hug.

"I'm sorry. Please don't be mad at me."

Nash's cane clatters to the porch as he braces himself on the doorway and his other arm instinctively curls around Teddy's shoulders.

"I ain't mad."

Teddy pulls back to look him in the eyes, anxiety written over his features. "You're not?"

He's even with Nash's nose now. He used to think Teddy'd never get past his chin. When did that change? How much else is gonna change while he's not around to notice?

"Yeah, I'm… I'm not mad. Sorry I yelled."

Teddy shakes his head and ducks down to collect Nash's cane. "I yell all the time. It's only fair, right?"

Nash accepts his cane. "I suppose," he says, even though he doesn't agree. Teddy might be okay giving in to his temper, but for Nash, there's a different standard—genetics he can only beat if he keeps a close handle on his emotions. Teddy can just be Teddy, but Nash has to be very, very careful to make sure he's always Nash.

Teddy steps back to let him through the doorway. "Where were you going? I'll go with you."

Nash forces an ironic smile and sinks down onto the porch swing. "I was goin' to see you and say sorry for bein' an ass. Now that's out of the way, I suppose I'm free to do whatever you want."

A curious relief relaxes Teddy's shoulders from around his ears. "Yeah? What if I want to show you a new program on my computer? I coded it myself."

Nash steels himself for the long, painful trek up a dusty gravel road after all. "Then I'd say let's go."

That night, while he's soaking his aches away in the bath, he can't help thinking of all the things he and Teddy are going to miss out on. He'll never know if Teddy gets another growth spurt or what he'll sound like when his voice drops. They won't get to go to high school together or take off on a road trip once Nash gets his license. All the new movies they'll never watch together, all the new people they'll meet as Just Teddy and Just Nash, never again Teddy and Nash.

There's a part of him that hopes it won't be forever. Part of him that thinks he'll see Teddy again, if only because he can't imagine not, but he can't believe it. He knows from hard, painful experience that there's nobody up there lookin' out for him. Maybe they'll keep in touch at first with a phone call every day after school like Teddy said, but Teddy's going to North Carolina, to a school for people like him, to a city like the one he lived in with his folks before they died.

It's like Deliverance was just a pit stop before Teddy got

called back to where he belongs, and Nash will always be here, with the same kids he's been growing around his whole life. It won't be his fault, but Teddy'll drift and drift until the day comes that he forgets him entirely.

It's with this thought in mind that he tries to think up a list of everything he wants to do before Teddy's gone. He stays still and thoughtful while the water grows cold, but the only thing he can think of is getting Teddy to the top of that mountain.

Which leads to a different kind of list. He has until August to get the bike running. That should be enough. He'll make sure it's enough.

CHAPTER ELEVEN

Fundamental

It's been dumping rain for two whole days, but Nash has hardly noticed, except for when he has to jog between the house and the garage to eat and pee. The pounding on the tin roof is the best kind of white noise—steady and loud enough to block out the world.

Perhaps too good at blocking out the world.

Teddy bursts into the garage, soaked through with mud splashed as high as his belly button, already snarling before the door can bang shut behind him.

"Are you avoiding me?"

"Am I— Obviously not? I'm working." Nash gestures at the dissected engine parts laid out around him.

"Oh, *obviously*," Teddy parrots with venom. "How come I haven't seen you for three days? 'Cuz you've been 'working?'"

"I— Yes." Nonplussed, he drops his arms to his sides. "How else am I going to get her ready in time?"

"Get *who*—" He cuts off abruptly as he finally takes in his surroundings, namely the blue plastic body of the dirt bike stacked on the counter over Nash's shoulder. "The bike? You're trying to get it running before…"

He trails off around the thing neither of them can speak aloud.

"Tryin'. She's gonna need some new parts, but I can't get to the scrap yard until the damn rain quits, so I'm doin' a lot of cleaning, mostly. Soakin' the rust off, that kind of thing."

"Oh." Teddy's shoulders slump in the absence of his anger, leaving him looking even more like a drowned rat.

Tentative, Nash says, "I suppose I should've called or something."

Teddy shakes his head, sending droplets pattering across the concrete. "Uncle Darren said I was being stupid. I just thought…" He turns on his heel. "I'll be right back."

Nash rocks forward as though to follow but is waylaid by the parts meticulously placed in a ring around him. "What're you doin'? It's really comin' down out there."

Teddy shoulders open the door, and a burst of rain blows in on a fearsome wind. "Give me ten minutes!" he calls back and then disappears into the storm.

Ten minutes for *what*?

His question is answered twenty minutes later when Teddy returns with Uncle Darren on his heels and each with a towel-covered bulk in their arms.

Nash closes the door behind them and hurries to clear a spot on the counter for them to put down their haul.

When Teddy rips off the towel and reveals his boxy old

computer, Nash nearly drops the plastic body casing he's holding. Teddy's chin is tipped up and his jaw is set like he's expecting a fight. Nash will never understand why that's always his first reaction. He's always on Teddy's side, even when it's a stupid place to be. Even when it means getting the snot kicked out of him and suspended for a week. He's *always* on Teddy's side.

"What'd you bring that here for?"

Teddy crosses his arms, drippier than ever. "Do you not want me here?"

Nash hazards a glance at Uncle Darren, but he's bent over a box of computer accessories towel-drying what the storm got with gracious concentration, like he didn't just hear the dumbest question in the world come out of his nephew's mouth.

"'Course, I do. I just don't understand what you expect to —"

"I *expect* to not spend the whole summer waiting around for you to surface from your pet project!"

"I got that. What I don't get is what you think you're gonna do with that thing."

Teddy sputters. "The usual— Whatever I— *What does it matter*?"

For what feels like the thousandth time, Nash snaps, "We don't have a computer, Ted." He forces his tone softer and adds, "That means no internet."

Uncle Darren's head pops up in Nash's peripheral, but he has attention only for Teddy as a complicated array of emotions swath his expression. Teddy turns away, but not before Nash catches the telltale pink in his cheeks and rimming his eyes.

Nash is already moving after him when Teddy pushes

open the door and is on his heels as he steps into a shock of rain, cold enough to pull goosebumps up out of his skin on impact.

He forces the door shut and catches up to Teddy's quick stride in a few easy bounds, then grabs his shoulder and pulls him around. "What're you doin'?"

Teddy whacks his arm and twists free. He plants his feet in the muddy drive. "I'm trying to spend time with you! But if you don't want me around, then I'll fucking—"

"Of course, I want you around!"

"You're not acting like it!"

"You're not talking to me! You're just jumping to conclusions and doing stuff without explaining. How am I supposed to know what's going on in your head?"

Teddy laughs, mean and spiteful. "Why do you need everything spelled out for you? It's not difficult math, Nash! You should be able to figure it out!"

He rocks with the hit that Teddy thrusts into his chest and, on instinct, catches his wrist. Teddy tries to twist free again, but Nash holds tight.

"Don't be an ass."

"You started it!"

"No, I—" He catches Teddy's other wrist as he tries to punch free. "You know this isn't math," he snaps. "You know I— If it was math, I wouldn't need help, but this isn't math."

Teddy makes a halfhearted attempt to break his grip, but Nash knows too well what he's like when he actually wants something, so he doesn't let him go.

"I'm *leaving*, Nash. We're *leaving*."

"I know. That's why I have to get the bike fixed before—"

"I don't care about the bike! I don't care about the fucking mountain! I care about—" He cuts off with a sharp inhale and screws his mouth into a puckered frown. His glasses slip down his nose and only then does Nash realize there are tears mixed with the rain on his face.

"I care," Nash says, barely audible over the rain. "I want... Let me do this for you."

Teddy shakes his head and sniffs hard. "What's it matter if we don't see each other all summer and then I—" He turns his head, jaw working silently.

"We'll see each other every day. I promise. I'll... I'll talk to Uncle Darren about moving the bike into your garage. I'll make it work, I swear."

Teddy frowns up at him. "Why is going up that mountain so important to you?"

Nash licks the rain from his lips. How can he explain? It makes sense in his head, but he knows it'll get all garbled and twisted 'round if he speaks it aloud.

It's to carry Teddy beyond the limits that he's always trying to overpower in the only way Nash can bring to fruition. But more than that, it's to make up for it. It's to make up for all the ways Nash wasn't good enough or quick enough or brave enough. It's to make up for all the times Teddy pushed closer, tested the boundary, only to be held at arm's length—not because the desire wasn't there, but because Nash was too scared to take the leap with him.

And, in the very back of his mind, there's a tiny niggling hope that up there, above Deliverance, far and away from anyone who might take issue with it, maybe Teddy will push near again, and he'll have the courage to meet him. Too little and too late, but there, nonetheless.

He releases Teddy's arms, but Teddy steps closer, eyes sharp through smeary lenses, searching for answers.

"Why's it important, Nash?"

He swallows. "It just is. I want... I want to."

Teddy stares up at him like he's trying to pry what he's not saying directly out of his brain. With each passing second, Nash becomes more aware of the way he's soaked through to his skin, the way Teddy is too—hair plastered to his scalp, clothes wrinkled and clinging, his glasses opaque as the wind howls and spits rain like pellets of ice.

"Teddy! Nash!"

Together they turn toward the porch where Uncle Darren is waving them inside.

Equal parts reluctant and grateful, Nash leads the way to the house where Uncle Darren greets them with fresh towels from the hall closet. Mama is nowhere in sight as they dry themselves off in the mudroom, but she must be nearby.

"I talked to your mom," Uncle Darren says. "We've come to an agreement, and we should have internet installed by the end of next week."

Nash blanches. "What?" He casts a glance at the interior of the house and says soft and quick as he can, "We can't afford that."

Uncle Darren matches his tone but speaks calm and slow. "Don't worry about who's paying for it. That's for adults to work out."

He wants to laugh. In what world are finances not his concern? Certainly not this one. Not when Mama makes it a point every other week to loudly bemoan how much the government takes from her paycheck; how much is immediately gone thanks to the mortgage, the water bill, gas, electric, and keepin' him and Jo fed and clothed as they grow quicker than they have any right to. Not when he has to pick up work around town to be able to afford the extra textbooks required to keep up with Teddy and his internet. Not when he has to skip lunch a few times a month to make the money stretch until Mama gets paid and can refill his and Jo's account with the school.

Uncle Darren drops a heavy hand onto his shoulder and squeezes. "Why don't you boys run and get changed into something dry? You won't mind finding something for Teddy, would you, Nash?"

He shakes his head. "'Course not."

He can count on one hand how many times Teddy has been inside his house and it never gets less strange having him follow along in his wake. Mama isn't in the front room or the kitchen when they pass through, and for that Nash breathes a sigh of relief.

Teddy was there for the aftermath of Daddy's grand finale, so he fully knows how awful he was before he split, but Nash has kept Mama's particular brand of nastiness under wraps enough that Teddy doesn't know the full picture of it, and Nash intends to keep it that way. The last thing he needs is Teddy taking up another crusade against his unfortunate parentage. Mama is sure to be pissed as hell that he's costing her money and bringing their troubles to the neighbor's attention. He doesn't need more problems kicked up by Teddy's moral compass.

Upstairs, Nash opens the door to the room he and Jo share and finds his sister sprawled on the floor on her belly with a stack of loose notebook paper and a pile of colored pencils.

She doesn't look up from her drawing of what looks like a humanized pegasus with rainbow hair. "Finally tired of making moon eyes at your lover?"

Nash freezes in the doorway as heat floods his face so fast it hurts. Then Teddy crashes into his back, and Jo looks up. Her eyes flare wide as they lock on Teddy, but he's too busy rubbing his nose and grumbling to notice the drawing.

She scrambles to bury it in blank pages and demands, "What are *you* doing here?"

Teddy leans around Nash. "We got tired of making moon eyes at each other and now we need dry clothes."

A vicious grin cracks across her face. "I was talking about Nash and his precious bike, but if the shoe fits." She collects her things and stands. She looks Nash in the eye and raises her eyebrows. "Are you going to block the door all day or...?"

He sidesteps to let Teddy into the room and doesn't look at him.

As Jo glides past she whispers, "He thinks of you as his lov—"

He shoves her out the door and slams it on her back, but they still have to listen to her cackle all the way down the stairs.

He keeps his face turned away from Teddy as he digs through his dresser, pulling out clothes at random—a hoodie, a pair of sweatpants, a long-sleeved shirt, athletic shorts, a flannel. He pauses with his hand on the top drawer. He wants socks and dry underwear. Should he... Teddy would appreciate underwear too. It's a weird and uncomfortable thing to share, but he knows he would hate sitting around in wet underwear.

Before he can overthink it, he grabs two pairs of socks and two pairs of underwear, then he drops it all in a heap on the bed.

"Pick what you want."

He doesn't watch Teddy rifle through the pile. Instead, he returns to his dresser and pulls out a pair of jeans for himself and a T-shirt. When he can't kill time shoving his clothes around any longer, he shuts the drawer and turns around.

Teddy is standing beside the bed with a lump of clothes held carefully away from the dripping wet clothes on his body.

It's only then, when Nash sees the bashful blush tinting Teddy's cheeks and his downcast eyes, that he realizes how quiet he's been since Jo stirred up her trouble.

His stomach twists. He doesn't know how to deal with this. He doesn't know how to put Teddy at ease without... Without revealing something he's not ready to have scrutinized or without lying about something he feels is as fundamental as breathing.

He clears his throat. "D'you wanna change here? Or I could change in the bathroom if that's better."

Teddy shrugs. He doesn't look at him. "We could both change here, just turn around and... Yeah. Unless that would make you uncomfortable."

He's tempted to run away, to change in the bathroom and use the time alone to get his head back on straight, but... Teddy still hasn't looked at him and he's never seen Teddy shy before. He worries that putting that distance between them will send the wrong message. That it'll tell Teddy something he doesn't mean, and he's already jumped to enough conclusions today.

He clears his throat. "No. That wouldn't— It won't make me uncomfortable."

Finally, Teddy meets his eyes. He's frowning like he doesn't believe him. Or perhaps like he's trying to read into what Nash isn't saying again.

Nash sighs, all at once exhausted with the unspoken

game. "We're just changing from wet to dry, Ted. Quit lookin' at me like I'm a puzzle, would you? There's nothin' weird about this."

A hesitant smile curves Teddy lips. "Nothing at all?"

Nash hesitates. He's honest by nature. He doesn't have the energy to concoct some kind of fabrication that he then has to keep up or else get caught. It's so much simpler to be upfront. And with Teddy... Well, there are few things he keeps from Teddy.

"I've never changed with someone in the room before. That part's kinda weird."

Teddy laughs airily. "Yeah, me neither. It's okay if you don't—"

Nash shakes his head firmly. "You're my best friend. I trust you."

Teddy's eyes are bright, all shyness gone, as he says, "I trust you too."

Later, while Teddy gets his computer set up, Uncle Darren looks over Nash's progress on the dirt bike. He listens to his analysis of what needs replacing, what he can probably find at the scrapyard, what he'll need to buy new, and how he can scrape together the funds for it. He looks pleased at first, but he turns sad toward the end.

When it's all laid out, he sets Nash's chore list aside and softly says, "You're too smart for this little town, Nash. I wish we could bring you with us."

Nash doesn't know about that. This little town is just as much a part of him as he is it. He's got the same rot making roots in his tissue and curling around his organs—too much to cut away without taking something vital. Maybe then, it's for the best that Teddy's getting out before he turns out like him. Maybe everything is going the way it should.

CHAPTER TWELVE

All he ever wanted

What do you want most?

There's a week of school left, and the essay question is meant to be a gimme. A quick couple of paragraphs to get them thinking, to hone their writing skill before they all duck out for the summer and neglect to even touch another pencil until August. If he was a handful of years younger, it would have been.

To be left alone.

That's all he ever wanted. To coast out of sight of teachers takin' pity on him for his wore-out clothes and awful grammar, and out of range of their whispers about a neglectful home life. To be overlooked by his bastard father, unscolded by his bitter mother, and unbothered by his lonesome sister. *Alone* and *quiet* were all he ever wanted.

Now all he wants is for Teddy to stay. He wants Uncle Darren and Aunt Julie to change their minds, to see how tore up he is over the impending move, and to decide their happiness—his and Teddy's—is more important than some fancy city education.

It's a fantasy, and he knows it.

He also knows he can't just write "Teddy," for his essay and expect that to pass uncontested. They already get ribbed for how close they are. The last thing he needs is to get sent to the guidance counselor to talk about appropriate relationships between teenage boys.

At worst, he could end up shipped to some kind of correctional summer camp. At best, it would give the other kids something more to give them crap about. No, not them. Him. Next year he'll have to deal with it all on his own—no use giving them more ammo. Especially ammo specially designed to shoot straight for his heart every time.

He doesn't write the essay. When Mr. Parkland comes 'round to collect, Nash only shakes his head and shrugs off his teacher's frown when he pauses at his desk, as though drawing everyone's attention will make the essay suddenly appear.

Disappointed, Mr. Parkland clicks his tongue, collects Teddy's essay, and moves on.

"What'd you write about?" Nash asks Teddy later under the cover of the end of the day scramble.

Teddy doesn't answer, just looks at him long and serious like Nash should know without him having to say it. And he supposes he does.

"Quit looking at me like that."

Nash snaps back to reality. The bike's engine is strewn around him in pieces, but he doesn't remember what he was doing with it all. He's distracted by Teddy, perched on a tall stool at the counter, his computer casting a greenish glow over his features.

Nash *was* trying to memorize the way Teddy's hair sticks up out of the cowlick on his crown. His fingers are itching for a pen, even though he's never been an artist. That's all Jo.

"How was I looking at you?"

"Like I'm dying." Teddy jabs at his keyboard with unnecessary force. "Or already dead."

Oh.

Nash drops his gaze to the parts neatly arranged in front of him. "Sorry."

Teddy pushes back and forces his stool to spin. It does so with a *screech* until he's facing Nash. He crosses his arms. "Just tell me."

"Tell you what?"

"Whatever's bothering you."

"You already know."

"It's more than that. You're being all…" He waves a hand at him, "—*stony*. Just tell me."

Nash's frown deepens. When did Teddy get so good at reading his silence? He used to obliviously blitz past Nash's dips in mood, none-the-wiser.

"Come *on*, Nash. Spit it out already!"

He works the words around his mouth before he finally

admits, "I don't have any pictures of you."

"What?"

"I don't— Someday I'm going to forget—" He cuts off as his throat goes tight and his voice threatens to pitch.

Someday he's going to forget everything. How Teddy looks, how he sounds, their inside jokes—everything. He knows because he's already forgetting his dad. The shape of him is there, but his face is faded and muddy.

He doesn't want that to happen to his memories of Teddy, even though it doesn't matter. Unlike his dad, Teddy is going to change. Six months from now, he could be five inches taller and growing a peach fuzz mustache. In a year, he could sound like a man. In five, he'll be unrecognizable. The Teddy he knows, the one looking back at him right now, will be erased, only living on in whatever foggy fragments withstand the corrosion of time.

It's not enough. Just the thought of it makes his chest tight with panic.

"I'm not *dying*," Teddy says. "We're going to see each other again."

"You don't know that." North Carolina is so far. He'd never make it. And Teddy... Once Teddy gets a taste of the city and technology and progress, there's no way he is ever coming back to pollen and dust and Nash.

Teddy hops down from his stool and stalks up to the opposite edge of the ring of parts on the floor. "Yes, I do because I'm promising you right now. You'll be seeing me again. Believe it."

"Did you just quote your cartoon at me?"

Teddy scowls. "It's an anime, and it's really good. You're just a hater."

"They spent the entire episode going around the room

watching people think and make weird faces."

"And how are you any different?"

"Fuck you."

Teddy smiles. "I shouldn't have started you on that episode. It's way better when you know the story and the characters."

"Sure, it is."

"I'll get you to watch it someday and then you'll see."

"Well, you're runnin' outta somedays. Best get convincin'."

He loses his smile and turns serious. "I told you, we're going to see each other again. And in the meantime, I'll call every day. You'll see."

Nash doesn't say anything as Teddy returns to his computer. As much as he'd like to believe Teddy, in his experience, when someone walks out of your life, they don't call, and they don't come back.

CHAPTER THIRTEEN

On top of the world

Sputtering and spewing, the bike cranks to life. Teddy leaps with a whoop, but Nash waits until it drops into a steady chug before he smiles in satisfaction.

"Quick test run around the drive?"

Teddy pauses collecting his backpack. "Both of us?"

"Yeah. That's the whole point, remember?"

He straddles the bike and Teddy climbs on behind him. Nash worries they'll be too much weight for the suspension, but the bike barely sinks under Teddy's added mass.

They nearly tip in the driveway when Teddy leans too far into the turn but he corrects quickly, latching his arms tight around Nash's middle, and they finish a wobbly donut.

"Up the hill and back!" Teddy cries in his ear.

Nash is happy to comply and spits dirt as he tears out of the driveway and Teddy crows in his ear.

The bike passes their tests, and he's lighter than he's felt in months as they tear their way up the mountain, following an old trail he hasn't set foot on since dear old dad gifted him a lifelong limp. The temperature drops as they enter the tree canopy, and the air turns rich and fragrant. If he's not careful, the tires slip on the bed of pine needles, but he finds if he keeps a steady hold on the throttle, they churn right over them, smooth as butter.

What was an hour hike on foot takes them ten minutes. They exit the canopy onto a sunlit outcrop that overlooks the valley. From here they can see Deliverance nestled in the foothills far below, and closer—nearly pressed into the base of the mountain and surrounded by rolling farmland on all sides—sit two houses squatting amid broccoli-sized trees. From up here, you can't see the hill that separates them. They appear to be solidly side-by-side.

Nash cuts the engine and lays the bike in the shade of the rock ledge that towers over their heads, then joins Teddy in the grass under a tall, knobbly sycamore with its white, barkless branches glinting in the sun. It's hot, even in the shade, and Teddy's gotta be feelin' it even worse considerin' he's got one of those hard, plasticky surgical masks on under his usual handkerchief to combat all the pollen 'n' crap, but he don't complain and his eyes are bright as he pulls a small plastic brick out of his backpack and tosses it to Nash.

"What's—" Nash turns it in his hands. A disposable camera. His heart leaps into his throat as he jerks to meet Teddy's proud squint. "What about you?" There's no time to get it developed by tomorrow.

He shrugs and turns his eyes to the sky. "Don't need it."

When Nash doesn't respond, he turns to him. "I could never forget you." He jerks his chin at the camera. "Show 'em to me when we see each other again. We can laugh about how different we are."

Before Teddy can react, Nash snaps a picture.

"Hey! I wasn't ready! Should I take my mask off?"

He winds the wheel to prep for the next picture. "No." He snaps another as Teddy glares. It's a familiar expression. He wants to remember it. He wants to remember every bit of him.

Teddy jerks his mask down around his neck anyway. "Just for the pictures," he says. "We'll make it quick."

"If you have an attack and I have to drive you back down the mountain after—"

"You *won't*. Come on, let's do one together."

"How?"

Teddy makes an exasperated face at him, and Nash takes a picture of that too. He winds the wheel.

"Okay, that's getting annoying. Gimme that thing."

"No. What do we do? Just guess?" He turns the camera around and leans toward Teddy as he snaps another picture.

"That was awful. We have to be closer. Like this."

He presses up against Nash, his cheek so close he can probably feel the heat that rushes up out of Nash's collar.

He hesitates, part of him thinking that capturing photographic evidence of Teddy's effect on him is a bad idea. Unless he figures out how to develop the film himself and designs a whole room for it, someone is going to see.

He takes the picture anyway. This is it. This is their last day. He might as well keep playing even as the ship goes under.

"I swear you're not getting half my head in on purpose,"

Teddy gripes from nigh two inches away. "Another one, but aim this time."

He's got no idea where the camera's even pointing as he snaps the next picture; he's too distracted by Teddy's nearness and the way the whole world is drilled down to this two-by-two square of dirt and the pair of them standing in it.

Teddy laughs and snatches at the camera as Nash winds the wheel. "What are you even doing? Let me see it."

"No, they're my pictures."

Teddy lunges, knocking into him, but Nash manages to keep the camera out of his reach.

"Just let me do one!"

It's difficult to say if Teddy steps on his foot and knocks him in the temple with his elbow on purpose, but it hardly matters because from there on it's a brawl, one Nash hardly participates in as he keeps the camera stretched as far from Teddy as he can while he clicks and winds the wheel.

Teddy is laughing as they tumble into the dirt, and Nash blindly snaps a picture as though it could capture the sound of it. Cross-legged, Teddy holds his mask over his mouth and nose until the dust settles, then drops it around his neck and kicks at Nash's ankle.

"You're a terrible photographer," he says, but it comes out so swathed in warmth and affection that Nash couldn't take offense even if he were the type.

He lifts the camera to capture the look on Teddy's face, but the button depresses funny under his finger. He lowers the camera and checks the count.

"Oh. Guess we're out."

"There are probably a couple decent ones in there."

"They'll all come out perfect."

The look on Teddy's face shifts from playful affection to

the one he gets when he looks at Nash all quiet and serious and wanting.

He regrets wasting so many snapshots capturing their wrestling match. Likely, it's for the best. Nobody could look at Teddy lookin' at him that way and take it to mean anything but what Nash knows in his heart.

Teddy reaches out and Nash's heart thuds against his ribs. This is it. This is what he didn't dare hope would come from this last-minute trip up the mountain. With a roll of film smeared with Teddy in his hand and Deliverance a speck at the bottom of the mountain, what's to stop him from reaching back and taking what Teddy has always quietly offered him but he was never brave enough to accept?

Except, when Nash lifts his hand, it's his wrist that Teddy clamps onto and his eyes turn hard as he says, "Come with us."

Nash stares at his empty fingers. "What?"

Teddy rolls up onto his knees and suddenly big earnest eyes are all Nash can see.

"Stow away in the moving truck. I'll sneak some snacks in there. Some water. Just come with us. What are they going to do when you're all the way in North Carolina? Drive you back?"

It takes a long beat for Nash's brain to tick over onto Teddy's train of thought. Stow away? Inside an un-air-conditioned moving truck? In Tennessee? In *August*? Maybe he's been reading that look wrong all these years and Teddy actually wants him *dead*.

Then Teddy pulls him in and looks him full in the eyes and says, "Run away with me," and Nash knows that, no, he's had the right of it all along and he's too far gone now to turn back even though it's a road he knows will end before it begins.

Teddy must know it too, right? He must know he'd never leave Jo alone in this place. With nobody but Mama? He has to know the plan they're throwing together like a last-minute casserole ten minutes before church ain't nothin' but a dream. But he's helpless to do anything other than play along. It's almost fun to concoct a runaway plan together. It's a fanciful distraction, better than sitting in silence waiting for time to run out, so he indulges it and eggs Teddy on with wilder and wilder contingency plans for how to keep from getting caught.

Heedless of Nash's silent plea for it to stay aloft forever, the sun sinks in the sky. He wouldn't mind if today never ended and tomorrow never began. He could stay like this forever—on top of the world with Teddy pressed up against his side—if only the universe would stop hating him for an evening and show him a small kindness.

But tomorrow can't be staved off with wishful thinking. Teddy is leaving, Nash is staying, and there's nothing they can do to change that.

The sun sets.

On the Spinoza's porch, Teddy hugs him—hard, swift, unexpected, and over before he can think to savor it. Then the door is opening, and Aunt Julie is ushering Teddy inside, asking about his lungs. Uncle Darren takes their place and asks Nash if he'd like a ride home, but he has his bike, so Uncle Darren squeezes his shoulder with a heavy smile.

"See you tomorrow. For once, Teddy will have to be up

at the same time you are."

It's the last time Nash sees Darren Spinoza.

The door closes and after a few minutes, the porch light turns off, leaving him alone in the dark.

He doesn't go home. Instead, he bikes back up the mountain in the fading twilight. It's stupid and foolish, and he nearly dies twice thanks to some roots he doesn't see in time and the slick layer of pine needles, but he makes it back to the top. He spends the night in the flattened spot of grass where he and Teddy spent the day.

Then, when the sun lights the valley, he watches with dread in his heart. It's too far to make out anything in detail, but he can clearly see the house, the old gray Toyota, and the moving truck. People are harder to identify, but he's sure the tiny indistinct figure that stops in the middle of the driveway —a pinprick of color against white rock—is Teddy. And he swears he's looking right at him.

Then another figure collects him, and the pair enter the car while the third disappears into the moving truck.

Nash holds his breath, chest aching, eyes wet, but no matter how hard he wishes, the two vehicles pull out onto the gravel and drive away from his mountain. He watches until they disappear around a turn. Then it's just him and the birdsong, staring down at an empty house with an empty feeling in his heart.

Also by Sarah B. Elisa

Wildflowers of Deliverance
Red, like my bleeding heart in your hand
Blue, like don't forget about me
Violet, like these delights (Coming soon)

Watch for more at SarahBElisa.com

About the Author

Sarah B. Elisa (she/her) grew up in Iowa with one foot in the city and the other on the back highway that leads to the small town where she was born. She writes stories centered around character growth and relationship dynamics—both romantic and platonic. She has a particular love for the queer and the working class, and finds joy in breathing fresh air into old tropes.

Watch for more at SarahBElisa.com